COVER UP

COVER UP

A TALE OF ART, INTIGUE, MURDER AND HIGH SOCIETY

DAGMAR LOWE

SleuthHound Books
Lake Worth, FL

SleuthHound Books
Cover Up
© 2007 by Dagmar Lowe
A SleuthHound Books Publication
First Edition

Sleuthhound Books is an imprint of and published by Humanics Publishing Group, a division of Brumby Holdings, Inc. Its trademark, consisting of the words "Sleuthhound Books" and the portrayal of a bloodhound is registered in the U.S. Patent and Trademark Office and in other countries.

Brumby Holdings, Inc.
12 S. Dixie Hwy, Ste. 203
Lake Worth, FL 33460
USA

Printed in the United States of America and the United Kingdom

ISBN (Paperback) 0-89334-425-7   9780893344252
ISBN (Hardcover) 0-89334-426-5   9780893344269

Library of Congress Control Number: 2006937164

All pieces of art at chapter headings are original paintings and drawings by Christopher Walker.

For my mother, A.B., with love.

Thank you Jeannie, Judy, and Gale for friendship and support.

And – of course – Harry.

*My grateful thanks for valuable advice to Nicholas Kirkbride and
Peter Johnson of Ackermann & Johnson Fine Art, London*

This is a work of fiction. Names, characters, places and incidents are either the product of the author's imagination or used fictitiously. Most of the places, like the Red Bar, happily exist.

TABLE OF CONTENTS

CHAPTER 1

"Oh. My. God!"

The words came like a tortured groan and were accompanied by the thud of books hitting the wooden floor. They were dropped by Daphne Caplan, who stood immobile in the open doorway to her husband's study.

Her eyes were fixed on the empty space above the fireplace, behind the large desk. She could just make out the contours of the painting that had hung there ever since she could remember, until last night. The room with its library-cased walls had contained only one other painting, and that was gone as well. With a glance she determined that there were no signs of a break in. The room was just as she always found it every morning when she entered it – except for those two sickening spaces.

Daphne looked at her wristwatch. The time was 8:20 on a beautiful morning in late May. The place: a comfortably appointed trophy mansion on the island of Palm Beach in southern Florida.

Daphne Caplan was not a woman given to melodramatic reactions. She knew there was no point in screaming, shouting, fainting or any other exaggerated response to the discovery of a theft. The logical step was to ring the police.

Without entering the study she turned back, leaving her books on the floor, and walked calmly to the telephone in the hall from where she made a short call reporting the theft. She gave her name and address and was assured that a police officer would be with her within the next twenty minutes.

Daphne's next task was a brisk tour of inspection of the large double sitting room and the dining room where the major pictures of her husband's collection were hung. Nothing was missing.

She then opened the door to the kitchen where her house-keeper was preparing breakfast. "Good morning, Betty", she greeted the woman who stood in front of the sink with her back to her.

Betty turned around: a heavily built woman in her sixties, tall with gray hair pulled into a tight, severe bunch at her neck. Bobby pins clamped in place any wisp that was at risk of stray-ing. Her large features lacked harmony but she exuded confi-dence and capability. Without interrupting what she was doing she acknowledged her mistress and asked, "Would you like some coffee now or will you wait?"

"No thank you, Betty," answered Daphne, "no breakfast for me yet. Tell me, did you notice anything unusual when you came in this morning?"

Betty looked up curiously: "No, why? Is anything wrong?"

"One could say that," responded Daphne dryly. "The paintings in the study are gone."

"What?" Betty now showed signs of shock. She quickly dried her hands and hastened to the study.

"Oh my Lord! I had no idea. When I came into the house at 8 o'clock, I turned off the alarm as usual. I didn't look into the study. The door was closed of course. I did go into the sitting room to open the curtains and everything was all right there. Have you called the police?"

"Yes, I have. They will be here any minute. Until then there's nothing we can do, really. I expect the others will come down later and will want breakfast. Get everything ready and we'll help ourselves."

"Very good, Mrs. Caplan. I'll get on with things. Call me if you need me," said the housekeeper, walking slowly back into the kitchen.

Daphne looked at her watch. Only five minutes had passed since her telephone call to the police. They would not be here for another ten at least. Her mind raced. Although she always tried to remain calm and controlled, it wasn't in her nature to wait passively when something so extreme had happened. But how could she relieve the tension, the anxiety? She had an idea. She took out a small address book and looked up a number. Then she made another call.

CHAPTER 2

"Good morning, Scottie!"

The door to Mrs. Molly Miller's kitchen opened sharply and the lady of the house appeared, leaning on a cane to take the weight off her bandaged left foot. The young man who occupied one of the two chairs at the breakfast table dropped his newspaper, jumped up and gave his aunt an audible kiss on the cheek. His disheveled hair and stubby chin were proof that he had only just risen in some haste. As a further concession to the early hour he wore a dressing gown and was barefoot. He clearly felt at home in his aunt's oceanfront apartment in Palm Beach.

Molly, who settled herself opposite her nephew, was perfectly turned out as always. A woman in her early seventies she had long accepted that her body was too well-rounded and lacking in height to comply with the modern ideal of beauty. Yet she was generally considered a pretty woman with her broad, almost heart-shaped face and the kind of complexion that needed little cosmetic help. Her hair was full, glossy and never less than immaculate, thanks to a mutually rewarding relationship with one of Palm Beach's more pampering stylists. And those parts of herself that fail to flatter with age, she covered with expensive decorum.

In her reluctance to show too much flesh, Molly set herself apart from many other Palm Beach ladies in their seventies and counting. Her friend Lou-Ann was a classic example. A grandmother many times over and easily on the wrong side of eighty, she had just married again. But Molly wasn't sure whether this triumph, as it was considered by her many single girlfriends, happened because of or despite the generous exposure of her aging body.

Lou-Ann was much given to shorts or miniskirts which allowed full and uninterrupted views of her stringy, veined legs, sagging thighs and the inevitable mahogany colored skin speckled with liver spots. There was a lot of bosom too, to the point where the décolleté resembled a steep, murky ravine with savage fault-lines.

Molly sometimes shuddered when she caught sight of such contemporaries who still presented themselves like girls, though no word of criticism had, or would ever, pass her lips. Her own preference was smart but understated: knee-length skirts in pastel colors, her tops didn't show more than a modest cleavage and were never sleeveless. Improvisation played no part in her closet: every item harmonized, coordinated, and was finished off with tasteful, unexceptional jewelry, usually pearls.

To be pleasing but not memorable in her attire was Molly's target, and she hit it without fail, thanks to a wardrobe that may not have been exciting but was extensive. So it was lucky that the accident with her foot had occurred before Manolita, Molly's maid, had started on the Herculean task of packing up for her mistress' summer sojourn to Ohio, her other residence.

Molly lived in fear that her apartment's air system might break down because, should this happen in her absence, she knew that her clothes would pick up mildew from the hot, humid summers in southern Florida and be ruined. So she took precautions. Every year before leaving Palm Beach, she and Manolita packed up all her personal belongings ready for transport. That included dresses, coats, hats, shoes and even table linen.

After several days of feverish packing, the accumulated luggage took on awesome proportions: 5 trunks, 6 large leather suitcases, 4 hat boxes were the minimum, piling into Everest-like peaks surrounded by attendant hillocks in the shape of uncoordinated bags and containers.

Everything was sent ahead, together with the car, to Cleveland, where another helper was assigned to the task of reintegrating the Palm Beach chattels into the Ohio closets. Teased about the scale of what her friends called 'Molly's mountain', her defense was the even more extensive traveling closets of her friends. Diana Bentley, for instance, had added a whole wing to her already sprawling house just for the clothes: a room for day-time wear, another for the evening gowns, a hat room and a special cold room for the furs.

When asked, Diana readily admitted that she had few occasions to wear fur in Florida: only a very few cool evenings when the air-conditioning in the limousine was overactive. But, she added, it was indispensable in London where even the summers were often cold enough to warrant at least a stole. And, as Molly was pleased to recount, the entire fur collection went off to London whenever its owner did.

As always, this morning Molly's eyes rested with evident pride and affection on Scott Harding, the only son of her younger sister. That he was her favorite was something she only admitted to herself and with a somewhat guilty conscience. He had a younger sister, Abby, and there were other nieces and nephews, but Scott had always been particularly close to Molly and her lamented late husband Jim. The affection was mutual, and as a boy he had often spent part of his school vacations with them.

After Jim's sudden death Scott had made himself particularly popular by lavishing loving care and attention on his aunt. And now he had grown into a successful young banker in Manhattan: early thirties, smart, well educated. He had a law degree from the Sorbonne, an MBA from Harvard, he owned a condo on Sutton Place and could afford to rent a small but charming house in East Hampton every summer. Year after year he invited his aunt to visit him but so far she had always declined. She much preferred it the other way around, when her family came to see her, either in her home in Cleveland or in Palm Beach.

The Millers had been living in Florida during the winter months for many years, like so many well-off people from Europe, Canada and the United States who had spent the past century sheltering here from the cold. Things had changed of course. Eighty years before, the Rockefellers, Huttons and Dodges would have arrived well after Christmas in their private railcars, taking residence in Mr. Flagler's stupendous new hotels or renting a "cottage" (minimum five bedrooms, not counting the servant quarters). The ladies would have moved around the island in rickshaws pulled by black attendants and changed dresses three times before supper.

These days, winter visitors more often made for the big anonymous apartment blocks at the south end of the island, sometimes uncharitably referred to as the "ghetto" or "Gaza strip" due to its demographics, and walked about in jeans or shell-suits. And where Florida's snowbirds used to fly home on Washington's birthday, February 22nd, they now departed by the end of April (or the latest, mid-May) – leaving the year-round residents of Palm Beach, existent only since the invention of air-conditioning, to settle down to hot and humid but uncrowded summers.

Jim and Molly Miller had always been snowbirds, flying off in spring but returning to the same third floor apartment where she still wintered: on South Ocean Boulevard, a thoroughfare flanked on the western side by mostly characterless white apartment blocks and the ocean on the other side. It was a fashionable address because of its waterfront views and proximity to the so-called heart of Palm Beach, which means Worth Avenue and the Evergreen Club. The club was Molly's home away from home where she spent most of her time lunching, attending parties or playing bridge. In adjusting to Jim's death, she had developed the lifestyle not exactly of a merry widow but of a contented one who cherished the company of her friends and family.

But above all, she was a woman with a lively interest in human affairs. You couldn't exactly call her nosy, but she was a sharp observer and people tended to confide in her. On matters involving her, she had an uncannily good memory. Twice in the last few years, crimes had happened almost literally on her doorstep. And in both cases she had been able to contribute substantially to solving the case, cast to her own astonishment in the unlikely role of a Floridian Miss Marple, and finding it in equal measure thrilling and the tiniest bit undignified to be mixed up with crime. Even when you were on the right side of the law. She herself never alluded to these events but they had turned her, in the close-knit circle of Palm Beach island life, into a celebrity, at least for a while. She was only too glad when the next season brought fresh news and gossip.

"How did you sleep my dear?" Mrs. Miller asked her nephew.

"Absolutely fine, Aunt Moll'," was the answer. "I'm still of an age where I can crash any time and any place."

"I'm delighted to hear it. So far my houseguests have always been happy. You know how people buy comfortable beds for themselves but deliver their guests to lumpy mattresses? Shameful! Jim and I made sure to get a really good bed for the guestroom and Manolita takes pride in our linen. No well-run household should be without Egyptian cotton sheets, remember that! And talking about Manolita, I'd better call her later to see if she's all right."

Like so many in domestic service on the Florida coast, Manolita was originally from Cuba, and she had gone to visit her sister in Santo Domingo, an annual trip usually undertaken a few days after Mrs. Miller's return to Cleveland. This year, however, was different.

On the 10th of May, a few days before her intended departure, Molly had visited for the last time in the season Jean-Christophe, her flamboyant "hair artist" in the Royal Poinciana Plaza. His salon, a gaudy fantasy boudoir with gilded mirrors and dainty side tables, upholstered furniture and windows richly hung with burgundy velvet, always reminded her of a stage set she had seen for a performance of La Traviatia. Violetta, in her courtesan days, would have felt at home there.

As she left these operatic premises, her hair restored to something like the rich chestnut of her youth, it happened. Molly's shoe caught on a tilting slab of pavement and she fell, twisting her ankle and hitting her head on the ground. She was stunned, although not unconscious, from the shock and the piercing pain from her foot.

Cerise, the assistant hairdresser, had seen Molly stumble and was instantly at her side. An ambulance came promptly, and within a half-hour of the accident Mrs. Miller was safely installed at Good Sam — the Good Samaritan Hospital in West

10

Palm Beach — where she was treated with a most satisfactory degree of attention and competence.

An X-ray confirmed that the ankle was twisted and had suffered a hairline fracture. It had to be bandaged and she was told to rest. Luckily there were no signs of concussion. Her right hand, which she had scraped on the concrete, was inspected and taken care of. The doctor in charge persuaded Molly to spend one night at the hospital as a precaution. The next day she was released with strong advice to use a cane, to "take it easy" and return in two weeks' time.

At first Molly was appalled that this little incident should interfere with her annual plans for Ohio. But she soon accepted the unavoidable and, accommodating as she was, saw virtue in the change. The managing company of her apartment block in Cleveland had been refurbishing the building since Christmas, and everyone had just been informed that the work was behind schedule and not to be completed until June at the earliest. Molly had been dismayed at the prospect of returning to dirt, noise and general mayhem. By postponing her trip she would avoid all that. And she was even more pacified when friends assured her how agreeable life could actually be in Palm Beach after the season. To her pleasant surprise, she discovered that a good number of the people she knew would not in fact be leaving until July. Some even planned to spend the whole summer there. So perhaps it wouldn't be too bad.

Of course there was the small matter of Molly's "battle of the bulge" to be considered. The late Jim had had nothing but praise for well built women and frequently confirmed that she had no less than lovely curves in the proper places. But keeping said curves under control had sent Molly into a perpetual state of warfare. She had given up golf recently, tennis a long time ago, swimming spoiled her hair, and the idea of joining a gym was never seriously entertained. But she had found one simple and dependable weapon in her fight against the flab: white sneakers. This is to say, she walked. In central Palm Beach, between her apartment, the club and the Society of the Four Arts on Royal Palm Way, she never used her car. And exchanging her pretty pumps into sneakers for this modest exercise regime made her feel thoroughly good about herself.

For the foreseeable future there would be none of this. No sneakers, no walking. And the pain of her injured foot threatened other practical problems in the absence of the ever-solicitous Manolita, who instantly offered to cancel her plans for Santo Domingo, though Mrs. Miller wouldn't hear of it.

The problems solved themselves that same night when Scott, alerted by Manolita, rang to offer his commiserations, insisting that he should come and make himself useful during Manolita's time away. Fortuitously his boss had just urged him to take a long break after working himself into the ground (and to the point of illness) on a tortuous but profitable takeover deal. Pale, weak, and coughing, he had dragged himself day after day into the office. Now that the pressure was off, it was clear that he needed a vacation, preferably with sea air. This enforced rest he now proposed to spend looking after his favorite aunt. It seemed like a mutually beneficial arrangement and was settled with minimum discussion.

Since then, aunt and nephew had been keeping house in great harmony. Scott did the shopping, some of the cooking (which he enjoyed), and played chauffeur.

They always had breakfast, prepared by Scott, at home. It was nothing elaborate, just coffee, fresh grapefruit or orange juice, croissants or whole grain bread and marmalade.

Over her coffee mug, Molly glanced out of the window at a view which after 30 years still amazed and delighted her. The Florida sun was harsh on this cloudless early summer day.

Across the busy road, all noise suffocated by efficient double glazing, the deserted, pristine, buttermilk colored beach stretched uninterrupted to both sides. A glaring white wooden structure that served as a watchtower for the lifeguard thrust its frame across the impossibly blue water. If you swapped the blindingly azure swimming pools of California with the Atlantic Ocean of Florida, it was classic David Hockney as displayed in his celebrated pool paintings.

Scott looked up from his newspaper. "Would you like more coffee? I hope yesterday's bread is fresh enough. We're running out of orange marmalade – how about black currant jam?"

"That would be lovely, darling. Both, more coffee and the jam. What a marvelous housekeeper you are! You can give Manolita a run for her money. Well, almost…"

She smiled and he laughed, remembering the blackened swordfish recipe Scott had tried the other night with a less than perfect result.

"Don't let me keep you from your paper."

Molly reached for the newspaper that Scott had left for her. As usual he had bagged the Shiny Sheet, although she had lately begun to take the more sophisticated Palm Beach Post entirely for his benefit.

"Oh no," he suddenly groaned, "This is terrible. I just read the first obituary of a Palm Beacher who didn't reach the minimum age of 87. The poor devil died two years short of it. But still," he smirked, "the average age of the recently deceased — that is, in the last week — was a most gratifying 91, which is more or less in compliance with the official statistics. We won't complain about that. Tell me, Aunt Moll, what makes people enjoy such longevity here?"

"Well, yes, I grant you we specialize in longevity but there is a problem," she answered as if she had given it serious thought. "As you know people here don't drink, don't smoke, and apparently there isn't nearly as much sex around as some would like us to believe. So I can only assume however long they live it must seem to them even longer."

At this precise moment the telephone rang. The young man picked it up and answered with a friendly "good morning." He listened for a moment and then said, pressing his hand over the receiver, "Aunt Moll, it's the Quattelstick Funeral Home."

When he saw her alarmed face, he grinned and took his hand away. "Good morning Daphne, yes, she is here. By the way, thank you very much for last night. We had a wonderful time."

He listened again before he continued: "Thank you, that's very kind. Well, here she is. One moment please." He passed the receiver to his aunt, who assumed as alert a voice as was possible for the time of day.

"Good morning, Daphne, this is an early call. I should be ringing you to thank you for the lovely dinner last night." There was a short pause and then Molly gasped audibly. "Heavens to Betsy! I don't believe it. Just now? …And nothing else?"

Another pause.

"What do you want me to do?" She listened again and then spoke quickly. "Of course, my dear, I'll be delighted. Maybe I should wait just a little while until you all have made your statements to the police. Is it all right if I came in, let's say, about an hour and a half?" She listened again and then added, "You won't forget to call your insurance company, will you?"

She stopped again and then ended the conversation. "Don't upset yourself too much, Daphne, I'll see you very soon."

Scott had long put his paper away and gave every sign of curiosity. "What, what? Tell me! What happened?"

"Goodness gracious me," sighed his aunt. "Poor Daphne has been burgled. Well, the two paintings in the study have disappeared. There were apparently no signs of a break in. And only those two pictures are gone. She wants me to come over to her house in a little while. Could I persuade you to drive me to her?"

"You bet." The young man could not hide his anticipation. "Wow, how exciting! I live in the Big Apple and life is so boring. The moment I move in with you, Aunt Moll, Palm Beach becomes a hotbed of crime."

"Dear Scott, you should not be joking about something so serious. Just think what a nasty shock it must have given poor Daphne."

"You said only two pictures were missing? What's the matter with the burglars in this town? We saw all these fabulous Impressionists in the sitting and dining room last night, and they weren't taken?" Scott displayed a practical if irreverent attitude to the incident.

"I am sure the stolen paintings were very nice," answered his aunt affably, "but I seem to remember that all the really valuable art is in the other rooms. Did you hear Daphne mention last night that the major pictures, like the Degas, are individually secured? An alarm goes off when someone tries to lift them off the wall."

"No, I didn't hear that, I was probably paying too much attention to the excellent hors d'oeuvres. So it seems the burglar was well-informed and took only what was relatively easy to steal."

Molly sighed. "It looks like it. But we will soon know more. Shall we leave here at 9:40? Then we'll be at Daphne's house at about ten. That should give the police sufficient time for their work before we turn up."

"Very good, Aunt Moll, your chauffeur will be ready."

CHAPTER 3

Daphne, sitting behind a small desk in her bedroom, looked out at the garden without taking in the view. Blind to the early morning sun basking on the water as well as the pastel freshness of her roses and the lush lawn still sparkling from its nightly spray, she could not suppress the memory of those empty spaces on the study wall. She was shocked that an intruder had managed to get into her house and puzzled that there were no other signs of this violation. She shuddered slightly. What an uproar this would cause! She was not overly concerned by the loss but hated the thought of all that lay in wait for her: the police, insurance people, press coverage…Thank God her friend Molly would turn up shortly. Hers was always a voice of reason, calm and comfort.

Daphne was a tall slim woman whose youthful looks and enviable energy belied her age, which was 62. But she was unconcerned about this and readily admitted it, which invariably caused surprise and even disbelief. Most people took her to be at least ten years younger. And of uncertain origin. Born and raised in London, she had spent the major part of her adult life in the US but was still English in many ways. There was the clipped accent she had never lost and never tried to. A healthy irreverence for appearances, fame and fortune set her apart, especially in Palm Beach where so many women spent their life in the pursuit of youth and acquisitions – be they husbands, jewels or real estate.

She had the dewy complexion of a typical "English rose" and looked her best with a minimum of make up. Perhaps her greatest assets were her startlingly blue eyes, which she emphasized by wearing tops, scarves and often large hats in the same color. She knew what suited her and dressed well: Donna Karan and Armani by day, Oscar de la Renta and Carolina Herrera (both of whom were friends) by night. She liked the elegance (and, yes, the sex appeal) in their creations. And she had a weakness for extravagantly expensive shoes, a remnant of her upbringing. Her mother had impressed on her the vital importance of footwear in the belief that English men were shy and tended to cast their eyes down, especially when talking to young ladies. Shoes, accordingly, might be the only thing about the girls they noticed.

Her husband had teased her endlessly with her "Englishness" but he really quite liked it, including her passion for growing roses, the novels of Jane Austin, English breakfast tea and making her own orange marmalade.

Daphne's marriage to Sol had been unusually happy. They were so very different in age, background and interests, and both had willfully strong characters. But rather than clash, the contrast had enlivened and stimulated their relationship.

The most surprising aspect of their union had been the beginning. Thirty-six years earlier, Daphne was a young journalist working for a British broadsheet in Fleet Street after taking a degree in French and Italian. She was formally attached to the lower echelons of the news desk. But being ambitious, capable and willing to step in wherever needed, she often found herself covering for one of her more experienced colleagues in other departments, even when she lacked specific knowledge of their subject. And so it was on the day she was destined to meet Sol Caplan.

In those days Caplan, twenty years her senior but in his circle considered a relatively young man, was already a successful financier. His father had set him up comfortably in business, but Caplan Junior surpassed everybody's expectations. At the age of forty he had created a property empire, mainly in Manhattan. He also made regular headlines on the sport pages when yet another of the yearlings he bred and trained in Kentucky won a race. On top of that he had already laid the foundations of an art collection for which he would become universally envied and praised.

The finance editor of Daphne's paper had set up an interview with Caplan but was then unexpectedly taken ill. His deputy had unchangeable commitments. So an urgent SOS went out to Daphne. Unperturbed, she gave herself a ten minute crash course in finance and had barely the time to read a brief biography of Caplan before she set off to meet him at his hotel, the Savoy.

The hotel concierge rang to announce her arrival and came back with the message that she was to meet the financier in his suite. Daphne had to knock three times at his door before she heard a strong male voice with an American accent calling her in. She opened the door and found a man, half-dressed, hopping around barefoot, clearly and comically in distress.

"Christ Almighty! Where are those bloody socks? Help me, will you? I can't find any socks. I am going to kill that maid of mine when I get home. I pay her more than a managing director and she can't even pack an overnight bag for me," he groaned.

Sol Cantor was a tall man with a shock of prematurely gray hair and looked impressive to Daphne despite being dressed only in his underwear, with a half buttoned shirt hanging down and a tie loose around his neck. He was running back and forth between bedroom, bathroom and sitting room. Daphne, not certain what to do, tentatively opened the top drawer of the tallboy in his bedroom. Inside were three pairs of brand new black socks. She picked one up and held it triumphantly in the air.

Sol Cantor snatched the sock away from her and declared, "You are a goddamned genius, woman!" while putting it on. Before he had time to step into the trousers that he now took from a hanger, he suddenly looked at her for the first time. "Hey! Who are you? You didn't come to help me find my socks, did you?"

Daphne laughed. "No. I am from the newspaper. I came to interview you."

Sol grinned. "I didn't know your paper had such pretty journalists. Sit down! I'll get us something to drink."

Sol and Daphne did not leave his suite for forty-eight hours. Their meeting was an example of instantaneous, unavoidable and irrepressible combustion of love and lust. Caplan was separated from his wife, with whom he had a little boy. Daphne was married to a lawyer who, when confronted with this new development, put up no resistance to a divorce. For five years they conducted a stormy but committed cross-Atlantic relationship before they got married in New York one fine spring morning.

Sol continued with his whirlwind pursuit of business and pleasure in several continents. Property, horses, opera and paintings were his passion, in that order. He was clearly a complicated character. He could be amiable but his partiality could not be depended on. He had a ruthless streak but had never strayed—or at least, had never been discovered to stray— beyond the line of legality. He had few friends and innumerable acquaintances. He was ambitious and acquisitive but his contributions to charity were legendary.

Sol was a man of contradictions. He was talkative and occasionally boastful, but nobody knew better than Daphne that in many (usually the most important things) he was secretive. He entertained generously but abhorred intimacy. And he enjoyed practical jokes that just occasionally could be embarrassing or uncomfortable for those at the receiving end.

The first of April, otherwise known as April Fools' Day, was an especially bad time to be near him, as one of his employees, newlywed, discovered on the day in question. This unfortunate young man received a note from his wife to say she'd had left him. When he raced home he found that her belongings had gone. He couldn't get in touch with her because she was out of town and Sol had ensured she got no messages. The poor man was in complete despair and bewilderment until everything was explained as a joke. It was one occasion when Daphne felt her husband had gone too far and she forced him to make generous reparations.

Daphne was the love of his life, which neither of them ever doubted. But if she wanted to see a fair amount of her husband, she had no choice but to join him on his constant travels: Chicago, Los Angeles, Kentucky, Sydney, Paris, and London. Early on they decided that there was no space for children in the sort of life they led. As time went by, their annual calendar was more and more determined by the racing, mainly in France and England, and by the program of the world's opera houses: the Met, La Scala, Covent Garden and Glyndebourne. Somehow Sol even managed to fit into this crowded schedule visits to his favorite art galleries and the major auction houses, another area of life where he had been cautious and successful with the choice of his advisers.

They tended to change. But one man who had influenced him for a long time was Stephen van Dreesen, an art dealer with an excellent eye although the galleries he had owned over the years had never been especially successful. Blessed with more artistic knowledge than business acumen, his dream of a Manhattan gallery had never come to pass.

Sol acknowledged Stephen's superior understanding of art but this was mixed with the slight, almost imperceptible contempt of someone who had made money for someone else who hadn't. Stephen, on the other hand, admired Sol's success, was probably envious, and unconsciously began to copy his friend. At first he had no choice but to enter into the spirit of practical jokes and after a while he too started playing pranks on people.

Daphne and Stephen had always enjoyed a good working relationship which had become closer in the last years of Sol's life. Stephen, with his gallery in Miami, had often come to Palm Beach to show them works of art, advise them or just to keep them company.

In Daphne, Sol had found an educated and sophisticated partner who shared his interests even if she could not always match his enthusiasm which was, like everything about him, larger than life. She enjoyed the traveling and the opera: what could be more pleasurable than to watch Angela Gheorghiou die of consumption in a Covent Garden La Bohème, or to waft across the Glyndebourne gardens for a black-tie picnic on a Mozart night? But when they finally slowed down, which did not happen until Sol was well into his seventies, Daphne sighed with relief. As she confided to a friend, "I have seen enough Toscas fling themselves from the battlement to last me for the rest of my life."

The same went for the races where, having led the winning horse around the paddock for the umpteenth time, she could think of nothing more pleasant than to sit at home and watch the sport of kings on television. As for art, she was certainly appreciative and knew her good fortune in being surrounded by it. But after they had amassed more fine paintings than could be displayed in their various residences, she felt it was time to stop.

Daphne was delighted when Sol decided to give up the Faubourg St. Honoré flat and the pied-a-terre in Knightsbridge. He had cut down on their visits to Europe when the Concorde went out of business, despising private planes as ostentatious. So they divided their time in his last years between the duplex on 5th Avenue and their house on the island of Palm Beach. As he got older and more frail, Sol chose to remain mostly in Florida, which suited Daphne to perfection. As much as she had enjoyed the metropolitan buzz when she was younger, nowadays she treasured the peace and quiet of the island, her sports (golf and tennis), her bicycling, gardening and walking.

But her idyllic life with Sol was not to last. Eight months ago he had passed away after a massive heart attack. She missed him very much, but his absence was slowly turning from the raw pain of the early days after his death to a bearably dull ache. And being an undemonstrative, reasonable woman, she had soon made an effort to engage in life again, seeing her friends and pursuing her interests.

From the early days of their marriage, Daphne had been involved in their art collection and caring for it now was her pleasure and duty. Not only did she like pictures, she liked Stephen van Dreesen. Naturally there was nothing even vaguely emotional about their relationship; Sol, after all, remained a forceful presence in her heart. Nevertheless, it was agreeable to be in the company of an attractive, intelligent man who valued her and, given the slightest prompting, would have courted her.

So far, alas for him, he'd found neither the opportunity nor the encouragement.

CHAPTER 4

As the first shock of her bereavement wore off, Daphne would remember with a wry smile how often she had joked about the prolific number of rich, man-hunting widows in Palm Beach. Now she was one of them – well, at least a rich widow, if not exactly of the man-hunting variety.

Having house guests seemed a logical first step into this strange, new, unattached life. Invitations were issued and promptly taken up. Several friends from England, two from New York, had come and gone. And then her goddaughter Lucinda had arrived.

Lucinda's mother Ruth was the youngest in a family closely connected with Daphne's in England. And although there was an age gap between the two, Daphne and Ruth had always kept in touch and made every effort to meet whenever the Caplans came to Europe. Daphne had happily agreed to be godmother to her friend's daughter and when she heard that Lucinda, after finishing school and completing a wild gap year of traveling, planned to study at Parsons School of Design in New York, she offered the girl a holiday in Palm Beach to give her an insight into the American way of life.

This had been gratefully accepted; but Ruth, although she loved her daughter dearly, felt it only fair to give her friend a word of warning. In a series of long transatlantic phone calls Daphne had been briefed to be a watchful guardian to the young girl. Lucinda, who was intelligent and attractive, had been a cause of worry since leaving school. Her parents felt that she drank more than was good for her and they didn't always approve of her choice of friends. So Ruth was only too delighted to remove her daughter from the temptations of dirty, dangerous London with its all-too-enticing pubs and clubs: the quiet life in Palm Beach would be perfect for her. But she impressed on Daphne the need for strict supervision, early hours and everything that constituted healthy living.

Two weeks ago, Daphne had sent a car to Miami to collect the young girl from the airport. She was a pretty, slim girl of 19 with long, dark hair, charming brown eyes and dressed according to the latest London fashion in sneakers, a T-Shirt, and jeans that were tighter and lower slung than Daphne would have thought possible. Lucinda had a great liking for T-shirts with unusual imprints; on arrival she sported a red top with a jungle image on the back, accompanied by the words The lion sleeps tonight. Daphne took that to be a reassuring message for at least the immediate future.

She had made a great effort to entertain her young guest. They had driven around the area, to the Museum of Modern Art in Fort Lauderdale, to shop in Boca Raton's Mizner Park and have lunch at Max where Daphne introduced her goddaughter to the delight of sweet potato fries. They had eaten ice cream at The Breakers, pizza at Cucina and key lime pie at Ta- boó. They went to the cinema and visited friends in Vero Beach. A couple of times Daphne had taken the girl to the Evergreen Club for lunch and to the Beach and Tennis Club for games and barbecues, mostly to meet other youngsters.

Lucinda had been polite but remained unresponsive. She seemed happy to spend her days sunbathing by the pool, reading glossy magazines and listening to her iPod. Daphne, who took her guardianship seriously, was a little worried. The girl seemed too docile. Maybe she was exhausted from her social life in London. Or maybe she was just biding her time before she could shortly fling herself into the New York party scene.

There was another girl in the house and Daphne had hoped they might keep each other company. Ewa came from Poland and was going to be a student in New York this summer. But the two girls did not hit it off: they were too different. Ewa was a much more mature girl who spent her free time preparing herself for the work that lay ahead of her at the Institute of Neurolinguistics. She had successfully finished her undergraduate studies in Prague and had come to take up a scholarship for a postgraduate study at Columbia University. The university in Warsaw had approached Daphne in the hope she might be able to organize a place for Ewa where she could spend a few weeks acclimatizing to a new life in the U.S. before embarking on her studies in New York. Sol had been a generous donor and sponsor to various universities, among them Warsaw, and it was not unusual for Daphne to be approached for help. She was so impressed by what she heard and read about the young scientist that she decided to invite her into her own home for a few weeks.

It had been made clear to Ewa that she was a guest and welcome to do as she liked. But Ewa was either too shy or too proud and had, at her own request, assumed the position of a sort of au pair girl. Rather than move into one of the luxurious guest bedrooms she had asked to stay in the much simpler maid's room behind the kitchen. She seemed to enjoy helping Betty, and the two of them could often be found cooking together, which gave Ewa a welcome opportunity to practice her already quite impressive English. She hardly ever joined Lucinda at the swimming pool and seemed reluctant to be seen in her rather old-fashioned black swimming costume. She was, it had to be said, dumpy; not short but definitely overweight, which she tried to hide by wearing long, wide skirts or a shapeless overall. Her eyes were hidden behind thick lenses and her flaxen hair was tortured into two stiff little plaits that gave her the unfortunate appearance of a serious, plump extra in The Sound of Music.

Daphne had tried, tactfully, to guide her toward a more flattering appearance, offering to buy her new clothes, to take her to the hairdresser, but Ewa had so firmly declined her efforts that she gave up. So the two girls, although only a few years apart in age, led very different lives at the Palm Beach home they shared: Ewa dusting, gardening or cooking when not at her books, and Lucinda lounging most days by the pool in a tiny bikini, lost to the world with headphones firmly clamped around her ears. Then, yesterday, two more houseguests arrived.

Daphne had not been looking forward to these latest, albeit temporary, additions to her household. They were Paul, Sol's son from his first marriage, and his wife, Sarah. Daphne had always made an effort to get on with Paul, who was a shy, pale child of six when she first met him. Unfortunately he was very different from his ebullient, charismatic father and took increasingly after his spoilt, weak mother, whom Daphne saw for the first and (hopefully) last time at Sol's funeral.

Paul was amiably limp in character and looks. Although barely forty years old, he had developed a pot belly and the soft blond hair over his blandly handsome face was diminishing. He had teetered haltingly through school, completed an undistinguished college education and, through lack of any talent and interest, ended up on the fringe of the Manhattan business world, scrabbling for deals entirely on the strength of his father's name. Several times he had lost more than he possessed, until Sol, tired of bailing out his unfortunate offspring, set him up with an adequate allowance on the condition that he "retired" from business.

Paul's wife, Sarah, had been chosen for him by his mother whose deeply ingrained snobbery was the most dominant and least attractive of her many unlovable character traits. Although neither distinguished nor well off, Sarah and her family made much of their heritage (they claimed to be direct Mayflower descendants) and connections (a cousin had been governor of Nebraska). This allegedly illustrious lineage, together with a conventionally pretty face, were sufficient for Paul's mother to find Sarah a desirable match for her son who, with his marriage, replaced one smothering, despotic female for another.

They had no children which Daphne considered a blessing. Sarah claimed to be too fragile to undergo the vigors of pregnancy and childbirth but the true reason was her fear of broken nights and stretch marks. The couple lived an itinerant, empty life mostly in New York, in pursuit of pleasure, parties and celebrities. Sarah had once enjoyed a short-lived career as an interior decorator to some of their society friends; and her precipitous retirement was not so much caused by lack of taste than moral judgment. It was whispered that cash and checks had fallen into the wrong hands, leaving angry clients to demand their money back and Sarah to withdraw in haste from the professional scene. Whenever their bank balked at the growing overdraft, Paul and Sarah cut down on expenses by wrangling an invitation to stay with one of their wealthy friends or relations, which had often meant Sol, but now meant Daphne.

The thought of this unattractive couple descending on her easy life had filled Daphne with foreboding for days. In their company she felt anxious, even in her own home. She hated the way Sarah called her 'Dephnee' although perfectly aware of the correct pronunciation. She was made uncomfortable by Paul who followed her around trying to make polite, inconsequential conversation of a kind he thought required of him as guest and stepson. Above all, she felt critically observed as if Paul, and particularly Sarah, were constantly computing her expenditure on herself, her house and her entertaining. She told herself that she was probably neurotic and should calm down: exercise her store of charity and humor. But it didn't work. The couple tried her nerves and she had to engage every ounce of self discipline to remain civil.

Her gloom had lifted slightly when she heard that her friend Molly Miller had delayed her departure from Palm Beach. During the busy season they had not seen enough of each other and Daphne was determined to catch up now with her. Sol and Molly's husband Jim had known each other through business, and when the two women met many years ago, they had quickly become intimates.

And more good news: Molly's nephew, Scott, who was described to her as charming, handsome and erudite, was in town and could surely be roped in as an escort for either Ewa or Lucinda. Very quickly a plan was hatched: In order to avoid having to spend an intolerable evening alone with Paul and Sarah, Daphne invited Molly and Scott to join them for dinner.

At the last minute their circle had widened even further. Deborah Ferolito called to say that she had arrived in Hobe Sound, a small resort some 40 miles from Palm Beach, where she was staying with friends for a couple of weeks. Deborah had been Sol's secretary for many years and she had become a popular, trusted family friend. Daphne was delighted at the prospect of seeing her again and instantly invited her to join the party. The motto in the circumstances was: the more the merrier.

30

It had been a memorable evening. Daphne had taken great care with the choice of food and the table decoration. After consultation with Betty she had decided on a cheese soufflé as a starter, one of the housekeeper's specialties, then a poached salmon with new potatoes, spinach and fresh, white sweet corn, followed by a dish of mixed red berries with a choice of cream or ice cream.

Daphne's three major reception rooms all opened out from the spacious hall and overlooked the garden. The dining room was unusual in that it had been turned into an octagon by built-in cupboards set at an angle in all four corners. The curtains were made of the same pale yellow silk that covered the walls. As in the sitting room, the focal points were the pictures: serious pictures, among them a Corot landscape, a dancer by Degas, a still life by Le Sidanier and two portraits by Matisse and Modigliani. Sol's main interest had been the French Impressionists but his collection included also a few more modern masters; so there was a Dali, a Rothko and a Francis Bacon.

The room was a magical sight at night when it was only lit by candles and frame-lights over the paintings. Daphne set the table herself; it was one of the few domestic tasks she enjoyed. As usual she left its fine English mahogany uncovered. All it needed were white organza place mats, sparkling silver and crystal and a huge bowl of white, yellow and pink roses from the garden.

To Daphne's slight disappointment, Ewa had declined the invitation to dinner. The girl had so earnestly implored her hostess to be allowed to help Betty that a refusal would have been cruel. So they had been seven: Paul and Sarah, Molly and Scott, Deborah, Lucinda and Daphne herself. Since this was not a formal dinner, Daphne saw no objection to having an odd number of guests and more ladies than men. She had long ago decided that it was the quality of a guest that was important – charm, knowledge, humor- not the gender; and she would rather invite extra women, if they were desirable company, than men, who so often had a much narrower range of interests.

The evening had been a success, she felt; nobody had disappointed her. Scott had made polite conversation with Lucinda who, not surprisingly, seemed bored - or maybe overwhelmed, being so much younger than anybody else. Daphne was gratified to see that Scott also attempted to include Ewa whenever there was an opportunity.

But the star of the evening had undoubtedly been Molly Miller who, although modest and not inclined to dominate the conversation, became the center of interest when Paul asked her about the murder that had taken place last year in Palm Beach. Molly reluctantly admitted that she was the one who unveiled the culprit. Scott and Daphne, of course, knew all about the incident, but the others were longing to hear what had happened.

"Look, there was nothing really particularly clever about solving the case", she countered. "I knew the murderer as well as the victim better than the police; and I had ample opportunity to watch what went on. In fact, that is the whole secret of detective work: look and listen."

One person not longing to hear any of this, though, was Sarah, who resented the idea of being overshadowed by an aging woman who, in her eyes, was neither slim, famous, rich nor elegant enough to warrant such attention.

Sarah was overdressed, as usual, in a long, black see-through skirt and a lacy top that revealed a bosom too perfect to be real. Suspiciously rounded mounts peaked out and up from her chest, remaining resolutely immobile even when the rest of her was in motion. It was a clear give-away in a town where cosmetic surgery was rarely discussed but freely applied and perpetually suspected. Too much jewelry didn't help. ("More baubles than on your average chandelier," as Sol once observed of his daughter-in-law.)

Repeatedly Sarah tried to return to the subject of her family and ancestry. When nobody showed great interest, she first sulked and then tried to flirt with Scott, who was amused but remained unresponsive.

"You know, Scott, it's an unexpected pleasure to meet a man in Palm Beach who isn't gay or old enough to be my grandfather," cooed Sarah. She fluttered her eyelids at him and continued in a hushed voice, "and who is single as well."

"I know", confessed Scott in a voice oozing with exaggerated false modesty, "my arrival caused a sensation." He made a strategically well-placed pause and continued in his normal voice. "So does the appearance on the social scene here of any single male, gay or not, who is still able to walk unaided."

Sarah, at a loss for an answer, giggled nervously. Her own husband, who couldn't have failed to notice the attention she paid to her neighbor, seemed not to care. By discussing with Daphne the latest movies and bestsellers he had scaled his own personal intellectual Everest for the day and was now happy to devote himself mostly to his dinner and his drink - more than was prudent. The only conversation he entered into with discernible interest was a discussion on hedge funds with Scott.

Etiquette decreed that Paul sit next to Daphne, who sought relief from him by making a mental list of all the nips and tucks Sarah was likely to have undergone in her quest for physical perfection. Her face showed the immaculate tautness that speaks either of the vibrancy of youth or the skill of a surgeon's knife. What else could be enhanced or false? The hair, just a shade too yellow, tumbling artfully down her back? The voluptuous lips, freakishly outlined with a dark pencil?

Daphne pulled herself visibly together and diverted her attention back to Paul. For the last ten minutes her contribution to their conversation had been an occasional nod and non-committal mono-syllable. The question he had asked her, brought her forcefully back to the present. "I say, Daphne", he wanted to know, "you don't feel too lonely here living on your own?"

Considering that this was their first meeting since Sol's death it was probably not an unreasonable inquiry but with Daphne it hit a nerve. Had anyone else spoken these words she would have probably been able to answer unperturbed. She might even have thought it a considered remark, but Daphne felt so on edge with Paul and Sarah, that she immediately recoiled. And his next sentence did nothing to undo the damage. "You can always count on us to come and keep you company."

Daphne gritted her teeth when she caught an approving little nod that Sarah, who had obviously overheard them, gave her husband. Clearly the two of them had prepared this little statement for her benefit.

Daphne felt a wave of anger wash over her, then retreat and followed by the now all-too-familiar sad emptiness that sat like a lump in her stomach. Was it so hard to understand how she felt? She was perfectly happy on her own, looked after by Betty and now with Ewa and Lucinda in the house as well. It was Sol she missed, his energy, his intellect, his spirit. He was her soul mate. Daphne hated this overused expression but it was the only one she could think of to describe the close intertwining of their beings that she had found with Sol. Nobody could replace him, least of all this graceless, insecure, young man in the thrall of his shallow wife. That he was Sol's son was simply irrelevant. He didn't look like his father, didn't sound like him and certainly didn't have even a hint of his father's powerful personality and charm.

As if appealing for help Daphne looked to her friend Molly, who instinctively seemed to sense her need for reassurance. "Daphne has promised me to travel more in the future," Molly pronounced, addressing no one in particular. "If I am very lucky she might come and see me in Cleveland. I know this is not the greatest treat under the sun, but I have some darling friends and I dare say we would 'push the boat out' for Daphne... Don't laugh!" Molly turned with mock anger on her nephew who made haste to turn a wide grin into an equally mischievous smile. "And you, young man", she continued addressing Scott, "you'd better get ready and brush up your social skills. Because sooner or later Daphne and I will come and visit New York together. I long to see all the new shows and exhibitions. We could do some shopping, see friends...in short, I hope we'll lead the profligate life of extremely merry widows."

With an apologetic wink to Daphne, Molly felt she had done her part of lightening the general mood.

"That would be just delightful." Now Sarah, feeling on familiar territory, woke up and spoke. "My mother could introduce you to some really interesting people," she promised without realizing how condescending that sounded. Daphne was not the only one who couldn't decide whether to be scornful or amused. "Of course, we have a huge circle of friends ourselves. Have you heard of Patty-Lou Simmons?"

Nobody had.

"She is a really famous actress, she played the second lead in an off-Broadway production of...what was it again?...Paul, can't you remember?" Her unfortunate husband, who looked his usual blank self, received an icy look. "And we know a lot of writers and journalists. We even met Barbara Walters once at a cocktail party." This last statement was made in a voice ripe with gleeful triumph. The glint in her eye spoke equally of the attention given to her drink as of her certainty of having scored sky-high in an imaginary competition for social prominence. The people around Daphne's table were too well behaved to snicker.

It was hard to counter such a display of naivety and silliness and, therefore, best ignored.

This time it was Deborah who turned the conversation back onto safer territory. Daphne knew her as extremely good value in any company: she was intelligent, well-traveled and well-read. And now she realized that saving the situation was a matter of urgency.

"Daphne, I hope you will show me your roses when I come back some other time during the day. I have news for you: I have suddenly become very interested in gardening because I am toying with the idea of moving to New Jersey. I think I am getting a little old for the mood and tempo of New York. It's a town for the young. A pretty house with a little garden and membership in a good golf club seem suddenly very tempting."

This caused a torrent of comments. Whether pro or con, everybody had a view on Deborah's proposed plans and was keen to encourage or advise against.

Lucinda stared at the older woman in evident disbelief. Although she had only once, briefly, been to New York, she had the highest expectations. Was it not the center of the civilized world? A sliver of an island, Manhattan, reverberating with music, art, culture, clubs and bars... The city that never sleeps...excitement and stimulation without end... a daily chance of rubbing shoulders with the most famous people in the world. Due to her limited personal experience, she didn't feel confident enough to voice her opinion but Scott, sitting next to her, could read her like an open book. 'How can anyone even think of swapping this earthly paradise for a stupid suburban bungalow near a boring golf course? This woman is just so SAD,' was written all over her face.

"You could have a dog, couldn't you?" In an instant all this blasé boredom of the sophisticated London teenager fell off her and was replaced by the lovely excitement of a normal young girl that she basically was. "One of these adorable, tiny little lapdogs with a big bow in his hair that you can always take with you. I always wanted one of these but for my parents a dog isn't a dog unless it's a Labrador and he has to stay in an outside kennel." After this rather endearing outburst she quickly sank bank into the familiar gloom of the misunderstood adolescent.

Scott could barely suppress his amusement, about Lucinda and the rest of the company. This at least was a safe topic and worth pursuing for the peaceful entertainment it provided in this mixed group of people. And indeed everybody around the table had their own opinion on the relative merit of urban existence versus bucolic bliss. He himself could see the advantages of both ways of life. For the moment he still enjoyed the high-pressure metropolitan buzz, provided he could occasionally let off steam in the Hamptons, in Colorado or Florida.

This new-found subject carried them safely and almost amicably through the rest of the evening. Daphne noticed that of all her guests Deborah, apart from her heroic rescue attempt, was the quietest. The reason became evident when she asked for peppermint tea after dinner. She complained about an upset stomach and looked so pale that Daphne urged her to stay the night rather than drive back to Hobe Sound. Deborah gratefully accepted the offer and rang her friends to tell them not to expect her home until morning.

Ewa had dutifully looked after them all evening long. She had taken on the job of a maid, but had done it with skill and a smile, which pleased Daphne. Regrettably the girl had not changed out of her roomy overall. But Daphne introduced her to everybody and she ended up sitting with them after dinner in the drawing room where they had coffee and tea: an opportunity for Ewa to display her usual attentiveness to others. She had noticed that Scott – still in recovery from overwork – tended to cough, and she insisted on making him a soothing herbal tea, alternating with cough linctus from the first-aid cabinet. Daphne was amused to see her 'little duckling' suddenly so animated. There was either a hitherto undiscovered motherly side to her or she was not totally immune to male charm after all.

Scott, in turn, took great interest in Ewa's academic career and encouraged her to tell them about it. They all congratulated her on winning her scholarship and wished her good luck for her future life in New York.

It was ten-thirty when the party broke up, the usual time for Palm Beachers to go to bed. Due to their combined efforts, the evening had been relatively easy, comfortable and peaceful. Considering the mixture of guests, the disparity of their ages, backgrounds and interest, Daphne felt the party had been almost a triumph. She congratulated herself on a mission successfully completed. For tonight at least, she thought, God's in heaven and all's right with the world.

CHAPTER 5

Molly and Scott were slowly driving north, up County Road past Palm Beach's landmark hotel, The Breakers, and towards Main Street and Royal Poinciana Way. Just before they reached St. Edward's Church, where Catholic Palm Beachers worship, as had the Kennedys in their days, Molly called out to her nephew, "Do stop, Scott! Sorry, could you turn here into Sunrise Avenue? I want to buy some flowers for poor Daphne. I didn't bring her anything last night and I bet she could use something to cheer her up today."

Just in time he managed to swing the car to the left, inching his way towards the Palm Beach Hotel, opposite which Molly pointed out a florist's shop, next to Echo, the Asian restaurant.

Despite the unseasonable time of year there seemed to be no parking place. Sunrise Avenue attracted a fair number of shoppers as it offered a wide variety of services. Apart from the hotel and a bank there was a real estate office – always big business in a town mesmerized by property dealings — a French bakery, a hairdresser and a bicycle shop.

"Hang on, Aunt Moll! Parking isn't easy here," said Scott as he began to maneuver the gray Toyota into a rather narrow looking space. He moved forward and backward a few times, with only inches to spare. Then, when he was just about perfectly placed and pushed back for the last time, it happened. He used slightly too much gas and bumped, gently but noisily, into the gleaming black limousine behind them.

"Damn!" the young man exclaimed. "Someone is sitting in that car." He groaned as he saw a figure emerging in haste from the other vehicle. "Here we go," he murmured resignedly.

"Leave it to me, Scottie! You just stay there!" said his aunt, opening her door. With difficulty she stepped out, taking her cane with her, and turned to confront their nemesis. A rather large elderly man, with gray hair and a well-kept small beard, formally dressed despite the summer weather in a suit, was preparing himself for an acrimonious confrontation. He was busy inspecting the damage. And it must have disappointed him that not even the tiniest scratch showed on his car bumper, so clearly was he aiming for an argument. He had raised himself up to his full height, looking down with a red face and blazing eyes onto the short elderly woman smiling at him.

"What the hell does this young man think he is doing?" the man barked at her. "He crashed into my car. Has he no respect for other people's property?"

"I am so very sorry," responded Molly in a soft, well modulated voice. "He really should have been more careful. You are absolutely right of course. The driver is my nephew, you see, and he only tried to park his car here because I asked him to. I wanted to buy some flowers. I am afraid this is entirely my fault."

Slightly disconcerted, the man continued his tirade. "He should have been more careful. This is no way to park an automobile."

"I completely agree with you," continued Molly undeterred. "It is very upsetting and irritating for you to have your car damaged. I cannot apologize enough."

"Well", he began hesitatingly and sounding much less disagreeable, "it's good of you to say so. Luckily there is no damage."

"Still," Molly insisted, "I think it's deplorable when someone is careless with other people's property. This beautiful car of yours could have been ruined. And it certainly is a beauty."

"You are very kind." The blazing eyes now actually began to twinkle. "A little bump like this is not the end of the world." The man had started to look at Molly more closely and he seemed to like what he saw. "By the way, I'm Stephen. I just came here today to collect a tarte aux pommes at the French Bakery." He said it with an exaggerated, rather clumsy French accent and explained, unnecessarily, "That's apple pie for you and me. Could I perhaps buy you a cup of coffee?" he added after a second's hesitation.

Molly's face showed just the ghost of a small satisfied smile. "My name is Miller, Molly Miller, and the young man in the car, who by the way is extremely sorry for his misdemeanor, is my nephew, Scott Harding from New York, who is staying with me. Thank you for the offer but I'm afraid we'll have to be going. I am on my way to see a friend and I better dash to get these flowers. Well, dash as much as I can with this." In explanation, Molly raised her cane and tapped her foot.

She turned and gave the man a little wave. "Good bye and, once again, I'm very sorry."

Stephen made a formal little bow. "Goodbye. I hope we'll meet again. I'll be looking out for you."

Five minutes later Molly returned with her flowers. With a big grin Scott opened the door for her. "Well Aunt Moll, congratulations! That was a very accomplished little demonstration of applied psychology. You really know how to charm the birds out of the trees. You practically had that old boy eating out of your hand," he continued in mock reproach. "You should be ashamed of yourself."

"Shush, Scottie! Yes, that went very well. I have actually used this little ploy before and it always works like a treat. If I had contradicted our new friend I would only have fanned his fury. The trick is to show exaggerated regret when someone has a trifling but legitimate grievance and you take the wind right out of their sails."

"How did you ever require these skills of manipulation?"

"Elementary, my dear Watson." She chuckled. "By the way, did you know that Conan Doyle never used this expression? I read it the other day. It was invented when they made all these Sherlock Holmes movies."

Scott shook his head. "Don't change the subject. Really, I don't think I can leave you unchaperoned in future, my dear aunt, the way you turn men's heads. I don't know! Women these days just aren't what they used to be."

Molly gave him a cautious testing glance. He caught her eye and they both laughed. Without further incident they continued on their way to Daphne's house and arrived at the appointed hour.

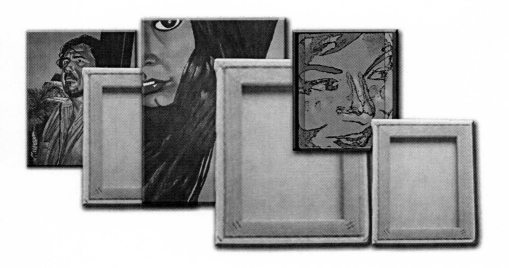

CHAPTER 6

When Scott turned into Daphne's drive he saw that three blue and white police sedans were already parked in front of the sprawling two-story house.

Mon Trésor had everything that Palm Beachers held dear in size and style. First, the original mansion was all of sixty years old, which made it a historic monument in Florida terms. Still more importantly, it was very large and boasted enough architectural features of a vaguely European nature to satisfy even the most ardent Luddites. Pillars abounded, windows were Georgian or even Venetian, a mansard roof echoed Gallic traditions, and to top it all a little bell tower above the garage that pretended to be stables evoked charming visions of the English countryside.

There was nothing original or unattractive about the house, and of course it looked as expensive and pristine as almost every property in Palm Beach. What Daphne called "overstated pretentiousness" had not bothered Sol. What had appealed to both of them immediately was the enviable position at the end of the island, where the Lake Worth water of the intra-coastal waterway met the Atlantic. All the major rooms opened onto an ample garden with a pool area that stretched down to the water. The view over the inlet in front, always busy with boats, was magical and left every first-time visitor breathless. In the distance rose the wide arch of the Blue Heron Bridge which connected Singer Island, on the right, with Riviera Beach in Palm Beach County. On the left this pretty picture was completed by little Peanut Island, uninhabited, palm-fringed, and a haven for boaters, swimmers and divers.

Mon Trésor was built close, with only one other property in between, to a small public dock, which marked the northern-most point on the Palm Beach Lake Trail, a recreation path much used by runners, bicyclists, and skaters. For Daphne this house, or rather this property, had been love at first sight, and she believed firmly that this was the only way to choose husbands or homes. The house, rather like her husband, was a tall order: unusual, over the top but special enough to put up with minor inconveniences. Sol was happy to fulfill her wish, and together they had turned Mon Trésor into a fitting showcase for their art collection.

Daphne had made sure that its grandeur did not exclude comfort and coziness. One of her major contributions was the garden, which she had made to look as English as the sub-trop-ical climate allowed. There were ample stretches of lawn, antique statues, some box topiary and a stunning rose garden. This had been another source of amusement to Sol. He liked to ask visitors whether they knew how the English maintained their immaculate lawns. Various suggestions were offered, but he could never wait to give them the correct answer, which he claimed he had heard many years ago from an old gardener in Yorkshire. "There is nothing to it," said the gardener. "Just mow it in the same straight lines for 500 years." To which Sol would add, "We've got a while to go, but you can see we're get-ting there."

Scott parked the Toyota behind the blue and white police cars. They were placed in complete symmetry around the semi-circular drive that ran along the front of the house. The main door stood wide open, and at that moment a uniformed policeman marched out of it, nodding absentmindedly to the recent arrivals before he jumped into the first of the cars and drove off.

Molly and Scott walked into the house, and through another open door they saw Daphne in the dining room, now turned into a makeshift office with a telephone, an open laptop and piles of paper on the table.

Daphne turned around when she heard them and beckoned them in, interrupting her talk with a tall man in a plain suit, probably another police officer.

"I am so glad to see you," said Daphne with a sigh but looking remarkably unruffled as she greeted Molly and Scott with a kiss. She relieved Molly of her bunch of lilies, thanking her profusely.

She turned to the man. "This is Detective Middleton from our local police station. Detective, these are my friends, Mrs. Miller and her nephew, Scott Harding, who were here last night. I know you want to talk to them."

They all sat down and Daphne continued. "Just for your information, Molly, the detective has already questioned Paul and Sarah, who are now at the pool, and Deborah, who went back to her room. She is still not feeling quite well. Apparently nobody heard or saw anything last night. Everybody slept soundly. Oh, the same goes for Ewa and for Betty, who lives in her own cottage behind the garage. Lucinda isn't even up yet. That girl has a remarkable capacity for sleep. I guess we'll have to wake her eventually. I'll see to it that she comes down when the detective has finished talking to you.

"I've told the detective that I gave everybody who stayed overnight the combination for the burglar alarm. There is a little box in the hall and you punch in some numbers to turn the alarm on or off. It only concerns the controlled entrance to the house and has nothing to do with the security for the good pictures in the other rooms. We had some mishaps in the past when houseguests felt like taking an early morning swim and off went the siren, followed by the arrival of the police. To avoid that I would rather let them know how to deal with the alarm, it's pretty basic anyway. Palm Beach, luckily, doesn't have a high crime rate, and Sol and I always kept a low profile socially. We never had any problems with security in the past. Anyway, I was just describing the pictures to the detective. I don't know how well you remember them?"

Molly shook her head and confessed guiltily that she had only a very sketchy recollection of a large nude.

"Well, why don't you stay here for a moment while I finish giving my statement? If you don't mind," Daphne added politely towards Detective Middleton.

He didn't mind and so she continued.

"Let's start with the little one between the book shelves over the walnut chest, opposite the entrance door. It is, or maybe I should say was, a Mediterranean landscape that Sol and I discovered and bought together on our honeymoon. The artist is a French painter, Blanche Camus, who has been dead for, well, at least thirty years. The picture shows the view down to a wooded bay in what I call Post-Impressionist style, very colorful, nice composition, easy on the eye. I think it was about 30 x 40 inches large, portrait format. By that I mean tall not wide; this is how they describe pictures in the trade." The last remark she added with a look to and for the benefit of the detective.

"You can see the size from where the pictures left a mark on the wall. By the way, Detective, we have photos and detailed descriptions of all our paintings. Some are with the insurance company and I believe Stephen van Dreesen, the art dealer who advised my husband, has copies.

50

"The other painting was perhaps Sol's favorite. It shows a naked woman stretched out on a sofa, one arm behind her head. Othon Friesz, a Frenchman, painted it and the picture is generally known as Reclining Nude. The canvas was approximately 50x40 inches in size, landscape format. Apparently Sol was so fond of the picture because he saw something of me in it." She paused and added. "As the model was quite stout I never thought that very flattering, but there you are. No accounting for taste. It was quite a fine painting, good brush stroke, but not a masterpiece."

"And because your husband was so fond of the picture he kept it in his study?" The detective wanted to know.

"I guess so," Daphne answered. "He had also determined in his will that the picture should remain in the family. Neither I nor my heirs were allowed to sell it for at least ten years."

"Isn't that rather strange?" asked Middleton.

"Maybe, but then my husband was an unusual man. He had firm tastes, a very strong will, and was used to reigning supreme, at least in his work. At home he didn't always get away with it, I am pleased to say." She smiled, adding, "Unless you have other questions, I'll leave you now. Would anyone like a cup of coffee?"

They all declined.

"Well, if you change your mind, just ask Betty, she's in the kitchen." With a nod Daphne left the room, closing the door behind her.

While Detective Middleton adjusted his glasses and rifled through his papers, Molly had time to study him. He was a stocky man, maybe in his mid-forties, with a weather beaten face and noticeably rough, reddened hands. He clearly was an outdoor man. A gardener? Golfer? Molly tried to imagine him in sports clothes and decided that water was his element, probably sailing.

"I heard that you were dinner guests last night here at the house. I understand of course that you did not spend the night here and were not in the house when it was burgled. Tell me, did you notice anything unusual during the evening?"

Molly and Scott looked at each other and shook their heads.

Molly took the lead. "Daphne is an old friend of mine, as was her late husband. We met through our husbands' business connections. Scott, who by the way had never met her before, came here for the first time last night. We had a very pleasant evening, but I cannot remember anything that would throw light on the burglary."

She hesitated for a moment and then asked, almost timidly, "Could we possibly see the study from where the pictures disappeared? Maybe that will jog my memory."

The detective obligingly got up and led them through the hall to the booklined room that had been Sol Caplan's sanctuary.

Everything was as Molly remembered it. The room was not particularly large, roughly square, approximately 15 x 15 feet, with a glass door on the left leading to the garden. A sizeable partners' desk, standing in a right angle to the entrance door, filled much of the space. Behind it was an armchair with its back against the fireplace. The mantel drew immediate attention because it was encrusted completely with seashells, very Palm Beach. The space above was empty, with a dusty rectangle outlining the shape of the painting that used to hang there. Two-thirds of the wall opposite the entrance door was covered with bookshelves. The gap in the middle was filled by a Georgian burr walnut chest of drawers. Above this glared another bare space, deprived of its painting. It made the room look, well, nude without the nude. Almost desecrated.

Making no comment, Molly and Scott glanced around and then, followed by the detective, turned back into the hall and through to the dining room to continue the interrogation.

"Can you recall whether any of the guests appeared nervous, on edge? That goes of course also for the members of the household, if you met them. I am thinking of the housekeeper Betty, and her helper, Ewa I think her name is."

"No great surprises there, Detective, as far as I can tell. My nephew will speak for himself. Paul, that is Mrs. Caplan's step son, drank quite a lot, and so did his wife actually. But that is nothing unusual, I think. Maybe Deborah was rather quiet, but she told us early on that she wasn't well. She looked pale and seemed glad that Daphne offered her a bed so she didn't have to drive back to Hobe Sound. She apologized profusely although there was no need, and she was the first to retire soon after dinner and a quick cup of tea."

Scott took up the description of the previous night from where his aunt stopped.

"We never saw the housekeeper because Ewa served the food and took the dishes back into the kitchen and all that. She was fine, a little shy perhaps. In the beginning she seemed nervous but later, when she sat with us, she became more relaxed. And then there was the English girl, Lucinda. She was rather quiet. I think she was plain bored because everybody else was quite a bit older, and she went to bed when Ms. Ferolito, that is Deborah, left."

"Thank you," said the officer. "Will you stay for a little while or are you going home immediately?"

"I would like to see whether I can be of assistance to Daphne," answered Molly. "If that's all right with you?" she added, looking at Scott.

"Sure, we can stay as long as you like," was his response.

As they got up to leave the dining room, one of the younger policemen suddenly appeared from the front door and whispered something urgently into Detective Middleton's ear. Immediately the detective rose, and with just a short word of apology followed his colleague out into the garden.

Molly and Scott looked at each other quizzically. They waited for a moment and when nobody returned they made their way into the drawing room to join Daphne.

Five minutes later the two policemen reappeared, and Middleton came straight into the drawing room where Paul and Sarah had now joined the others.

"I'm afraid I have bad news," said the detective in a loud voice, barely able to contain his breathlessness. "We've found a dead man in the garden."

CHAPTER 7

The first response to this bombshell was a shriek from Sarah. She leaped up screaming, "My God, how terrible! What happened?" Paul tried to pull her down but she resisted. "For God's sake, Detective, was he murdered? Was it an accident?"

Daphne also got up but forced herself to stay calm. Molly and Scott remained seated, looking at each other.

"Well, I don't think so. It seems the man died as a result of a series of blows to the head. He was probably hit with a heavy object. An ambulance is on its way but there's nothing anyone can do for him now. He's been dead some time. According to the papers, he had on him his name is John Poliakoff. Have any of you heard this name?"

The detective now was very businesslike.

Everybody in the room shook their heads. "That sounds Russian, doesn't it?" Molly asked.

"Or Polish," added Daphne. "Maybe you should ask Betty and Ewa?"

The detective nodded and Daphne offered to go call them. "I'll fetch Lucinda and Deborah as well. You will want to speak to everybody."

When all the nine people who were in the house had gathered, Detective Middleton asked the same question again.

Nobody seemed to know the dead man. Molly looked carefully at their faces. She thought she saw Ewa turning pale, but the girl apparently had nothing to say.

"At the moment," said the detective, "we don't know where the man came from and what he was doing here, but it will not take long to track him down. Can you please all stay here in the house or in the garden? I may have to ask you more questions."

"Oh, Detective," Daphne called after him, "where exactly did you find the man?"

"Halfway down the drive, going towards the house on your right. It's quite a dense part of the garden with trees and shrubs. That was enough to cover up the body, until we started a proper search."

The house was now bursting with activity. Some of the policemen closeted themselves in the dining room and made loud urgent telephone calls. Cars drove up, disgorging men in plain clothes and some in uniform. The front door was now kept permanently open. The gravel on the drive crunched under heavy shoes. Photographers unloaded their equipment. Forensic experts shuffled around. One man, who seemed to be a doctor from his black case, stepped into the house and was immediately shown to the garden, accompanied by an officer. Almost simultaneously an ambulance could be heard, arriving to take the dead man away.

After another half hour, Middleton came back.

"Well, we know now that the man lived in Miami and worked for an auction house. He seems to be of Polish origin. Next of kin are his parents, Oleg and Petra Poliakoff, who emigrated from Warsaw to the United States about thirty years ago and live now in San Diego, California."

Daphne and Molly's eyes were drawn immediately to Ewa, whose discomfort was obvious but only natural in the circumstances. That the murder victim was Polish was bound to have some impact on her. Maybe the name was even familiar?

After a moment's silence, Middleton continued, "I'm going back to the police station. It is possible that some higher ranking colleague of mine will take over this case, now that we are dealing with murder. There will probably be more questions to answer tomorrow morning. I am afraid I'll have to ask you all to remain at the house or at least in Palm Beach for a day or so. I must also urge you not to mention the murder to anyone. We want to notify the victim's family first. Meanwhile, if anything comes to mind concerning last night or the dead man, please call me at my office. I'll leave the number with Mrs. Caplan. Thank you all for your cooperation."

Everybody seemed a little calmer now, even Sarah, although she needed a second glass of brandy to steady her nerves. Betty and Ewa disappeared into the kitchen with a promise of lunch. They all claimed to have no appetite but Daphne, remembering her duties as a hostess, was sure that a slice of quiche and some salad would be welcomed.

Before they could troop out to the terrace where a table had been laid, the doorbell rang. Daphne stepped forward with a sigh to open the door. She cheered up instantly when she recognized their visitor: a very large man in his late sixties, tall and heavily built, with gray hair that was slicked back and a small, well-kept goatee. In front of him he held a rectangular, flat cardboard box. He spoke immediately with a loud voice.

"My dearest Daphne," he boomed. "I came as soon as I heard what had happened. I was in Miami, you understand, otherwise I would have been with you hours ago. Poor you! Poor, poor you!" He pressed the box into her hands and clasped her in a bear hug from which she freed herself laughingly.

Molly's eyes widened in surprise and she gave Scott a conspiratorial smile. The man was Stephen, the irritable car owner they had just met an hour or so ago. She noticed again how well dressed he was in his elegant khaki-colored linen suit and a pink shirt. He appeared more flamboyant than before because he now had a red silk scarf slung around his neck that matched a handkerchief bulging out of his breast pocket.

Daphne tried vainly to open the box and asked, "Stephen, what's that? You are not supposed to bring me presents."

"Who says? Since I know how fond you are of tarte aux pommes, the least I can do for you in your present difficulties is to indulge your sweet tooth." He turned around and cast his eyes anxiously around the drawing room.

"Now tell me, is the collection intact? Are all the really good pictures still here? Is it true that only the two from the study were taken?"

For the first time he seemed to notice now the other people in the room. He released Daphne and turned first to Molly. He looked baffled but recognized her immediately and seemed genuinely pleased to see her.

"My dear lady, enchanté to meet you again. Who would have thought that our paths would cross again so soon?" Stephen gave a deep bow and planted an air kiss just over the hand of an astonished and bemused Molly. When he noticed Daphne's surprised expression, he explained, "We met briefly this morning outside the French bakery, both engaged in purchasing gifts for our dearest Daphne: cakes and flowers."

He even managed to greet Scott with good grace. The young man used the opportunity to apologize in person for the trouble his careless parking had caused this morning. Stephen, all generosity and bonhomie, wouldn't hear about it and assured Scott that any misdemeanor, if there ever had been one, was long forgotten and forgiven.

Molly observed the little scene with interest and amusement. Stephen van Dreesen was clearly a mercurial character, quick to take offense one moment and all benevolent generosity the next.

The new guest greeted Paul and Sarah, who had both met him before with Sol. "Stephen van Dreesen is an old friend of the family," Daphne explained for the benefit of Molly and Scott. "He is a wonderfully knowledgeable art dealer, with a delightful gallery in Miami — you may have heard his name. Stephen advised Sol on his collection for many years. He really was a man of the first importance in terms of our art collection. We haven't met since he came to evaluate the pictures after Sol's death. I am very happy to see you, Stephen, although the occasion is rather unfortunate."

She invited her new guest to join them on the terrace.

Van Dreesen remained standing where he was and raised his arms, addressing Daphne with dramatic urgency. "Dearest friend, allow me first to feast my eyes on your treasure. Ah, there is our Degas," he declaimed, turning to the picture on the wall closest to him. He then made his way around the room and greeted each painting like an old friend. "Here is my beloved Le Sidanier and there you are, exquisite little Bonnard."

It was a theatrical performance but not without some charm, that was perhaps more appreciated by the ladies than by the two men present who exchanged a meaningful look. Finally van Dreesen plunged into an armchair opposite the ladies, as though exhausted by his own fervor.

"We must thank the good Lord that all these precious, priceless masterpieces are still where they belong. I cannot bear to think of them taken, violated, maybe damaged or destroyed. It is bad enough that the two pictures from the study were taken. Both of them are of course charming and dear Sol was very attached to them. A great shame, no doubt, but if I may say so their loss can perhaps be borne."

61

"Didn't you find the Friesz for Sol?" Daphne wanted to know.

"Indeed, I did. What a good memory you have. Sol and I had only just met. Let me think, that must have been more than thirty years ago! Nobody was interested in the Fauves in those days, and Friesz fetched very little money. I discovered the picture and mentioned it to Sol who snapped it up. A smart move, if I may say so. What a clever man! And so much missed," he added as an after thought.

He looked suitably distressed but his spirit revived again quickly when Daphne invited him to stay for lunch.

"My dearest Daphne, you are too kind. Nobody feels like eating and drinking on a sad day like this but we have an obligation to keep ourselves strong for what is ahead of us. We must hunt down the perpetrators of this dastardly deed."

Daphne knew this was her cue to tell him about the latest, much more dreadful crime that had happened so recently. She took him aside while the others at her instigation, sat down on the terrace. Molly, who observed them, saw that van Dreesen seemed genuinely shocked. Again he put his arm around Daphne, who did not seem unwilling to enjoy a small gesture of male protectiveness. After a while they joined the others who had already started lunch.

The meal was delicious, but a strange atmosphere of subdued horror, fright and disbelief seemed to hover over the little group. Molly, who as always observed everything and everybody with keen interest, was reminded of the Garden of Eden after the appearance of sin and shame. One bite of the apple and paradise had lost its innocence, forever. The only lighter note was struck by Lucinda's T-shirt. Today's message was Don't even try and, though this wasn't out of keeping with the general mood, it drew some smiles and teasing comments.

Much affected by the thought of the unknown man who had found death in her garden, Daphne was grateful for Stephen's efforts to keep up some sort of conversation. Scott supported him valiantly, fishing for suitable subjects. But Molly seemed preoccupied, more silent than usual. She was searching for an excuse to be alone with Ewa.

CHAPTER 8

Scott had been vainly trying for the last ten minutes to catch Molly's eye. They had been at Daphne's house now for quite a few hours and he felt it was time to leave. She was aware of what he wanted, but it suited her to ignore his efforts and increasing restlessness – to the point where Scott decided stronger measures were in order. He got up and stretched himself.

"I don't know about you, Aunt Moll, but I could do with a little siesta. May I take you home?"

Molly obligingly got up but immediately sank back with a subdued groan, blushing with embarrassment as the assembled company looked on.

"I am so sorry, Daphne, I think I have overdone it. My doctor asked me to keep this silly foot still and put it up as much as possible. I wonder whether I could rest for a moment before Scott drives me home."

Daphne was deeply concerned about her friend and immediately offered her own bedroom. The two main guest-room suites after all were taken up by Paul, Sarah and Deborah, who was now forced to stay at least another day. Molly accepted instantly.

"Please Daphne, don't leave Mr. van Dreesen alone. Perhaps Ewa could come with me and help me with that useless foot of mine." She looked at the girl who seemed uncertain of what to do.

"Give me your arm, dear, and we'll go upstairs," said Molly, who was not averse to taking initiatives. "Perhaps you could be an angel and check my bandage, which suddenly feels awfully tight." And with a conspiratorial look at Scott she said, "I won't be long, Scottie. Be patient with your old aunt."

In Daphne's bedroom she sank into a squashy pale blue armchair and called the girl to her side. "Ewa," she said gently, "please tell me what's on your mind." The trouble with the foot seemed to have temporarily slipped her mind. The girl looked flushed, hung her head, and remained silent.

"Ewa, in a murder case nobody can afford to keep secrets. The police will find out everything. It's better if you tell me now."

Tears began to well up in Ewa's eyes and she started to sob. Molly patted the chair next to hers, inviting the girl to sit down. She did so but it took a few more minutes before she was calm enough to speak.

"I'm not completely sure," she whispered, interrupted by the occasional sob, "but I think the dead man must be my cousin Yuri, I mean John. His name is John Poliakoff. In the family we call him Yuri, but his American friends call him John. After the policeman told us about dead person in the garden I tried to call Yuri on his cell phone but he didn't answer.

"Yuri was supposed to see me last night. He rang to ask whether we could meet, quite late. He wanted to give me something, for safe keeping he said. I don't know what he meant. He seemed so mysterious. I think he was worried."

"All right," said Molly, now satisfied, "slow down a little. Why didn't you tell Detective Middleton immediately that you suspected the dead man was your cousin?"

"I was so stunned," replied the girl miserably. "I was shocked and then frightened. I thought here I am, in America. I want to go to New York to study and how can I do that when I am involved in crime? I am so afraid to be sent back to Poland. This is such chance for me, to be here, and now I could lose it all." She started sobbing again.

Molly took her hand and stroked it gently. "Don't worry. I know this must have come as a terrible shock to you. Even if the dead man should turn out to be your cousin, I am sure you have nothing to do with his death and nobody will send you back to Poland. But I also know it's better if you come forward now and tell the police everything, believe me! Is there anything else you can think of? When did you last see Yuri? And how often did you meet since you came to Florida?"

"We met soon after I arrived, four weeks ago. I went three times to Miami to see him. Mrs. Caplan is very nice to me, but I felt a little homesick and lonely. Everything here is new and strange for me. Although I didn't know Yuri before I came to Florida, I felt comfortable with him and we could speak Polish together. He showed me Miami, South Beach and all that. He told me about his life and his friends and his work. He is very nice person, very intelligent. We both like reading, and he recommended lots of books to me. You know, he studied French literature. He is…I mean he was…." She broke off again, unable to control her grief, and started crying again.

Molly gave her time to calm down a little and after a while she continued asking. "When did you see Yuri, or John, for the last time?"

"Maybe a week ago. We made plans to meet up again to go to movie next time and he wanted to show me his favorite bar. We had many plans. But then he called to say he was busy. He sounded strange. I asked him what was the matter but he wouldn't tell me anything. All he said was 'don't worry, it will be all right.'"

Ewa gave a big sigh and dried her face with a large, plain handkerchief that she found in a pocket of her overall. Molly closed her eyes in an effort to concentrate and then she asked, "Is there anything else you can think of? You believe he was in some sort of trouble and needed help? Try to remember exactly what he said to you," Molly urged.

"Yes, there was something else," the girl recalled, suddenly alert, "but I don't know what it means. Just before he hung up he asked me strange question. What was it again? Oh yes, he said, 'Do you know Maupassant?'"

"Oh, and what did you answer?"

"I said, 'I have heard the name but I don't know any of his writing.' And then he said something like 'never mind. I call you again, soon.' Then he gave a strange sort of laugh but it wasn't funny, if you know what I mean, and hung up."

"And did he — I mean, call you again?"

"Yes, but not until yesterday morning, when he told me he wanted to come and see me. I asked him not to ring the doorbell, but to leave a message on my cell phone instead when he was near the house. That's why I didn't want to eat dinner with Mrs. Caplan and her guests. I needed to check my telephone from time to time, and I wanted to be able to step outside to speak to Yuri. But he never rang and never came. Well, it seems now that he came, but I swear I didn't see him and I never spoke to him again."

"My darling girl, all will be well, I promise you." Molly felt desperately sorry for this young person who was so far away from home and now had lost the only link she had in this country with her family in such a cruel way. "Leave it to me for the moment. I'll speak to the police and let them know that you have something to say after all. I am sure they understand that you were in shock, and it will be good if you come forward on your own accord. Shall we do that?"

Ewa looked up and gave the tiniest smile. She trusted the elderly woman next to her and so she nodded. "If you think so. I hope they'll understand. And thank you, Mrs. Miller, you are so kind."

"Now, will you help me down these stairs again, my dear?"

Molly was highly satisfied with the outcome of this little interview. Suddenly she was in a great rush to get home and her foot, miraculously, did not seem to bother her any more.

CHAPTER 9

For a man of Scott's youth, size and build he was surprisingly gentle when he maneuvered his aunt into the car, not forgetting her cane. Molly waved back to Daphne, who had insisted on seeing her friend out.

They were not even half way home, still north of the country club, when Molly could no longer suppress her yawns. "Oh dear, I am tired. Not that I had any physical exercise but things like this are so upsetting," she sighed. "Poor Daphne! What a terrible day for her! Being burgled is bad enough, but to discover a dead man in your garden is horrendous. I wonder whether the two incidents are connected. Yes, I would think so." She was mulling things over and Scott listened to her musings with interest and a smile.

"First there is the robbery. Well, I don't know about the actual chronological order, but this is how we heard about it. We don't actually know at this point whether the murder was committed before or after the pictures were stolen. My guess is it was after. I don't believe the two stolen paintings are great favorites of Daphne's, however much Sol loved them. And of course the insurance company will pay for them. But still, any burglary is highly disturbing. Just the thought that a stranger walks through your house while you sleep..." She shuddered.

Scott, who was concentrating on driving as slowly and smoothly as he knew his aunt liked, searched for the right words to comfort her. Actually he had found the robbery quite exciting but death, a violent one, was an entirely different matter and had to be taken seriously.

"Was Yuri the thief?" Molly had already told Scott about her little talk with Ewa. "Did he have an accomplice? Did they fall out? Was there an argument that led to a fight? Oh dear, I wonder what's behind all this. Let's go home as quickly as possible. I have to make some urgent phone calls."

A few minutes later Scott dropped off his aunt outside her condo building, and while he parked the car in the underground garage the porter helped her into the elevator. Today Robert was on duty – her favorite porter. Over the years there had been a number of "Bobs" working at 325 South Ocean Boulevard, sometimes even alongside Robert, who was the only one who insisted on using his unabbreviated name. So Robert it was.

Porters enjoyed a good life in Palm Beach. Most apartments were occupied by elderly ladies who, the odd cantankerous exception aside, made few demands and were usually grateful for even the smallest services rendered. Porters on night duty could generally sleep without interruption, thanks to the early-to-bed habits of the island. There were no late night revelers losing their keys or being sick in the lobby. And a modicum of efficiency, combined with goodwill and a suitably subservient attitude guaranteed tips that mounted up into a healthy income.

Molly always felt that Robert was a cut above his colleagues. That he was impeccably dressed and groomed went without saying. In his case the dark garb of his profession didn't so much define him as an employee, it rather enhanced his innate dignity into the gravitas more often associated with elder statesmen. In a measured, well modulated tone he spouted the platitudes that were expected of him. "Lovely weather today, isn't it, Mrs. Samuelson?" or "I hope your back is not giving you too much trouble, Sir."

Robert could be relied upon to supply a certain amount of news or gossip, as was expected; but Molly frequently wondered whether she was the only one who seemed to detect just the merest hint of mockery in his confidential reports. Occasionally she asked questions about acquaintances in the building with the intention of testing these suspicions, but so far she had always failed to reach a final verdict.

"How is Mrs. Sorenson these days?" she asked. "Or rather, Mrs. Markham I should say."

Lillian Sorenson, as Molly had known her for so many years, was the wealthy widow of a manufacturer of small but apparently essential car parts, which he had developed in his youth and skillfully marketed. She was in her eighties and in poor health, more often bedridden than not. But in one of her spells of relative well-being she had made the acquaintance of one Jon Markham, a man in his fifties who had come over to Palm Beach for the day from Boca Raton where he was visiting a cousin. Or so he said.

When his friendship with Lillian seemed to become serious, there was no shortage of well-meaning friends who uttered warning, pointing out that Jon was too young for her and could only be a gold digger. With magnificent recklessness she had cast all doubts into the air and made Jon her lawful wedded husband. When he moved his few possessions into her large, dark, lonely apartment, the strange marriage of two needy people began.

Barely a month later Lillian had a stroke, which forced Jon to find his own entertainment, leaving his bride in the hands of nurses and other caregivers. Jon had no choice but to turn to golf, tennis and card games to keep his despair at bay but insisted on dutifully visiting his wife's bedside at least twice a week. It was an everyday story of Palm Beach life, a standard situation with a predictable outcome.

Robert considered Molly's question about Lillian for a second and then answered with a fraction less restraint than was his habit. "Oh, not too well, I am afraid. I see Dr. Santiago come in for her every couple of days. She seems to have some very capable nurses looking after her."

After a meaningful pause he continued, unprompted. "Mr. Markham, on the other hand, is very well indeed. He just returned from a cruise. It seems his wife's worrying situation causes him much trouble and he needed a break."

"Really?" was Mrs. Miller's response in a flat tone but with sharply raised eyebrows. She suppressed any further comment, since she was now at her apartment.

She was just opening the door, Robert withdrawing with a deep bow, when the telephone rang. She managed to get to it, hobbling as fast as she could, before the answering system kicked in. A voice that was vaguely familiar to her said politely, "Good evening, Mrs. Miller." As soon as she heard the next sentence she knew who it was and a smile spread across her face.

"We haven't seen each other for a while," the man said.

"And I am so pleased to hear from you, Special Agent Gonzalez," she replied.

"Mrs. Miller, we have to meet. It seems we are yet again involved in a crime together. I have just been asked to investigate the death of John Poliakoff on the grounds of Mrs. Caplan's house. The local police would have dealt with the burglary but homicide combined with a possible interstate – or even international – art theft becomes a different matter, so the FBI has been called in. And, confidentially, I can tell you that the case would probably have ended up with us anyway. The late Mr. Caplan was not only a major player on the international financial scene, he also had government connections that I won't trouble you with. Suffice it to say he was an important man and we take a continuing interest in his affairs."

"How fascinating!" said Mrs. Miller, her interest picking up. "There is clearly a lot here that needs investigating. And I'm thrilled that you're the investigator on the case. I have all the confidence in the world that you'll find the answers we need."

"The Miami office seems to agree. They assigned me to the case immediately. My relationship with your police chief may have something to do with my placement. He and I have a history together. He's former FBI, you know."

"Yes, I had heard," Molly said. "But I didn't realize you two shared a history."

"We trained together at the FBI National Academy in Quantico. Did you know only one half of one percent of all law officers get to attend? He and I made it through the academic program with no problem but then came the physical training and that's something you never forget. I hope I'm not boring you; my wife always stops me when I bring up the subject. The guys who do it with you often become your best friends. The endurance and obstacle course is six and a quarter miles long – The Yellow Brick Road they call it – and to call it intense is an understatement. It took all of our physical strength combined with sheer will power and stamina to make it through. But we knew that if we did, we'd be ready for anything the bureau – or the force – could ever throw our way. We've come a long way since then."

"How fascinating! Some day you must tell me more about this," interjected Molly, her admiration evident in her voice. " Well, under the circumstances I am not surprised the chief is pleased to have you back in town and on the case. I'm sure he'll want to get you caught up right away on the details of the investigation. By the way, I have also some information that I would like to share with you."

She told him about her conversation with Ewa.

"Good, very good, that sounds like a significant lead," replied the agent. "It's almost certain that the two crimes are connected, we just don't know how as yet. This young lady, Ewa, has some explaining to do. I'll be at Mrs. Caplan's house in the morning to see you all. In the meantime, please don't talk about the homicide case to anybody."

"Of course not, Special Agent Gonzalez. But can you answer a few more questions for me, please? What was the cause of death and when did it happen?"

"The forensic evidence and autopsy agree that death must have set in no later than midnight. It appears that he was repeatedly hit over the head with a heavy, sharp object. Several blows were sufficiently serious to be the cause of death, some others were more superficial but strong enough to stun a man.

"We think the weapon may have been a brick, because there were some lying around loose near the spot where we found him, and they seem to have been disturbed. If this is the case, it's possible that the killer dropped the brick, the lethal weapon, afterwards into the water. We sent some divers out but they haven't found anything yet."

"Thank you. So we may not be dealing with a premeditated attack then? Could it be that two people had an argument; one grabbed a brick to hit the other; and then, finding his victim unconscious, decided he had no choice but to finish him off?" asked Molly.

"That's more or less how I see it", replied the agent.

"Is there any chance that the object was robbery? What did Mr. Poliakoff have on him when you found him?"

"No robbery as far as we can tell. He had his papers on him, a wallet with quite a bit of money and his car keys. My colleagues have located a Cadillac that was left in the parking area of the little public dock area near the Caplan house and the key fits. Let me see," he could be heard rifling in some papers. "Yes, I see here, the car was definitely his. That has been checked."

"I see. Thank you for that, Mr. Gonzalez, now I have some food for thought."

"I've just spoken to Mrs. Caplan and asked her to make sure her guests stay in her house until at least tomorrow, and that they do not talk to anyone about the dead man."

Molly once again promised the same for herself and Scott, and assured him that they would both be at Mon Trésor in the morning.

Excitedly she called out to her nephew, who had just stepped into the apartment.

"Scott, I don't believe it. The FBI has been called in for the murder case and my old friend, Special Agent Emilio Gonzalez, is in charge. A delightful man, you'll meet him tomorrow morning."

She then relayed the general content of her conversation with Gonzalez. Scott listened, bemused.

"OK Aunt Moll, so far so good. But please do me a favor and have a rest now. If you are a good girl and put up your foot I'll bring you a cup of tea at 5 o'clock."

"Oh, stop fussing, Scottie," said his aunt. "You have no idea how exciting all this is for me. I hate criminals and crimes but solving them is, well, invigorating. Listen, there was something I have to ask you. You are much better read than I am," she began.

Scott grinned at the admission that his taste ran to something a little more demanding than Regency love stories. Hers did too, in fact; but the image of Molly as a devotee of kitsch romantic fiction had become the stuff of family lore and he could never resist teasing her about it. Her invariable reply was that Georgette Heyer was a fine writer who "knew what women want." But not on this occasion.

"How familiar are you, Scottie, with the writer Maupassant? You must have read him when you lived in Paris."

"Maupassant?" repeated Scott. "Mais oui ma belle amie."

Molly's incomprehension told him that his little joke required explaining.

"Maupassant wrote a novel called Bel Ami. And another one with the rather lovely title L'inutile Beauté which translates as 'Useless Beauty.' Then there are his short stories. Why do you ask? Do you feel tempted to widen your literary horizon?"

"No thank you," replied his aunt firmly, "I'll stick with Barbara Cartland. But do you think you could get some books by Maupassant, in English of course? His best known novels and the short stories perhaps. I'll tell you why later."

"Okay Aunt Moll. If you are good and do as I say — resting that is — I'll run over to the Classic Book Shop and see what they have."

"And, sorry Scott, just one more thing. Do you remember that I told you about Marylou Baker and Sam Robertson?"

"Afraid not. Have I met them?"

"I don't think so. Sam is the son of Frank Robertson, the man whose horrible murder occasioned my previous encounter with Special Agent Gonzalez, and Marylou is his girlfriend. She owns an art gallery here in town which they now run together. They should be in Palm Beach. I'll phone them and see whether we can get together, maybe even later today. Would you like to meet them, Scott? They are a very attractive couple, more or less your age."

"Sure, why not," Scott readily agreed, "as long as you promise not to walk too much for the rest of the day…"

True to her promise, Molly lay down on her bed for a while, making phone calls. At 5 o'clock Scott knocked at her door and came in to bring her a cup of tea.

"Oh, Scottie, you are a darling. Thank you for that tea! I spoke to Marylou and she's happy to see us. She and Sam will be in the gallery until 6:30. I suggest we get there at about six. If we leave an hour later we are in perfect time for dinner at Ta-boó. My treat. What do you think? "

"Done, Aunt Molly!" answered the nephew promptly. "That sounds like a thoroughly decent plan to me."

At the appointed hour Scott chauffeured Molly up Worth Avenue and parked the car opposite the Evergreen Club. When she got out, Molly took Scott's arm, her cane in the other hand, and together they walked slowly into Via Parigi.

The Vias were the gems of Palm Beach: little pedestrian lanes designed as a fantasy Mediterranean pastiche by the legendary architect Addison Mizner. They housed restaurants, shops, galleries and a few luxury apartments. Where Via Parigi widened into a small piazza, the large windows of a yellow house displayed a number of contemporary paintings. This was Marylou's gallery, substantially enlarged since Sam Robertson had become her partner, in life as in business, a year earlier.

As they advanced, a dark-haired woman happened to look out and when she recognized Molly and her companion, she waved and opened the door.

"Molly, welcome! How lovely to see you. But what happened?" she asked pointing to Molly's cane and bandaged foot.

"Ah, this is nothing, a little accident. Have you met my nephew, Scott Harding?"

Marylou said hello and explained that Sam would join them shortly. Marylou Baker was a tall woman in her thirties with long dark hair and an open expression. A handsome rather than pretty woman in plain clothes, she came over as straightforward and direct, a relatively rare quality in her line of work.

"I am here because I need your expertise," said Molly, not wasting any time. "It's very lucky that I could get hold of you today."

"The luck is all ours, Molly. I had no idea you were still here so late in the season," said a voice behind her. Mrs. Miller turned around and gave Sam Robertson an affectionate hug. The two men were introduced and shook hands and Molly explained about her tumble.

Sam Robertson was a tall, boyish-looking man with startling blue eyes and long soft hair that flopped over his forehead. Molly had known him and his family for many years, since they had all moved to Palm Beach, but she only became real friends with Sam and his sister after their father was murdered. Frank Robertson had been killed on the Evergreen Golf course in Palm Beach; and although the police and the FBI, in the person of Special Agent Gonzalez, had investigated the case, it was Molly who had unmasked the killer. In dramatic circumstances.

Looking at her watch and finding it was well past six, Marylou locked the gallery door and they all sat down.

"Now, Molly, you said on the phone that you needed our expertise, as you so kindly put it. And since this afternoon was quiet, I had time to look up the painters you mentioned and make some notes. But what's it all about? You sounded mysterious. Or can you not tell us?" Sam wanted to know.

"Well," Molly started hesitatingly. "I can say just so much: It looks as if I've stumbled into another crime scene, entirely accidentally, I can assure you. Scott, why don't you tell what happened?"

"Okay, here we go. The day before yesterday my aunt was invited to a friend's house for dinner and she kindly took me along. Do you know Daphne Caplan?"

Marylou and Sam shook their heads.

"Daphne is the widow of Sol Caplan..."

"Ah yes," interrupted Sam. "Of course I've heard of Sol Caplan and his collection, but I've never met him or his wife."

"Well, that's the one. Daphne gave a dinner party in her house at the far north end of the island. There were other guests. Great fun, lovely house, nice food and all that. Everything was fine and dandy until this morning, when Daphne called early to say that she had been burgled during the night. Sol's famous collection, mostly Impressionists as you know, was not touched. The thief took only two pictures from the study and I think Molly wants to know more about them, or rather the painters."

Molly took over: "We spent the morning with poor Daphne. The police were all over the place, searching the house and garden, taking fingerprints, questioning everybody and so on."

Molly was very tempted to talk about the body in the garden, but she felt honor bound to keep silent and anyway, they would hear and read about it shortly.

"This is why I need you to give me some professional information. What do you know about the two painters? Let's start with the picture that hung over the mantelpiece. It was an oil painting of a naked woman lying on her bed. The artist is called, I believe, Friesz. An unusual name – was he French?"

"Yes, his full name was Achille Emile Othon Friesz, which by the way is Belgian though he was born and bred in France. He lived from 1879 until 1949 and worked in Paris, Normandy and in the South. In his early years, in Paris, he shared a studio in Montmartre, with various other painters including Picasso.

That was before they gained recognition, and a time when they were so poor that they sometimes paid for their food – and no doubt wine – with their own pictures." Sam had pulled out some notes which he consulted from time to time while he gave his explanations.

"Friesz started off as an Impressionist but today he's known mostly for his membership of a group called the Fauves, which means wild animals. The name was coined when they first exhibited in 1905 and shocked the world with their primitive techniques, their harsh outlines, lack of perspective, unnatural colors and so on. Matisse, Dufy, Derain, van Dongen, Braque, Vlaminck were the mainstay of this school. Most of them moved on into different groups and different methodologies. But Friesz got sort of stuck, continuing to paint in pretty much the same style to the end of his life.

"His colleagues held him in high esteem, but he never quite reached their stature and he's only become seriously collectable in recent years. Wake Forest University in North Carolina has one of his paintings, Paysage Provencal from 1914. And I seem to remember that I saw a charming nude by him…well, where was it?" Sam paused and then continued: "Is that what you wanted to know?"

"Yes, yes, thank you, Sam, very interesting. And what do you think his paintings are worth nowadays?"

"I did some research on that," answered Marylou. "A few years ago his work was relatively inexpensive but lately, as Sam said, Friesz has emerged from obscurity. I'd say that a good oil by him nowadays could easily be worth $200,000. Maybe more."

"And how easy would it be to sell one of his pictures?" Scott wanted to know. "I understand that sometimes a crazy collector commissions the theft of a work of art because he's desperate to own it — then it goes underground and may never resurface. But let's just assume the thief wanted to sell this picture. Could he get away with it?"

Marylou and Sam looked at each other. Finally she responded. "If someone brought me a painting by Friesz, I would not necessarily recognize it unless it was signed. In any case I'd certainly research it before buying and check the police lists of stolen art. Other dealers might not be so scrupulous. They would ask fewer questions, pay less money and try to pass it on for a quick profit. And then there is also the chance of selling it through an auction house. So well, yes, I think it would be possible to make money from a stolen Friesz."

"Thank you," said Molly, "that's really helpful. Now about the other painter, someone called Blanche Camus, a woman I suppose. Have you come across her?"

"Blanche Camus is another superb artist who still awaits adequate recognition. She too was French and lived from 1884 until 1968, pretty much a contemporary of Friesz. Her favorite subject was the Bay of St. Tropez, which she painted again and again in a late Impressionist style, very appealing, with a colorful palette reminiscent of Bonnard," explained Marylou.

"As it happens we have one of her pictures, but it's stacked away in storage at the moment. It is called The White Parrot and shows a big bird and a striped deck chair in a garden with a dog on the grass. You see her favorite setting, St. Tropez, in the background. We're asking $ 30,000 for it. It is one of our more valuable pieces and I like it very much. But as you can see, Blanche Camus is certainly not in the megabucks category. Yet.

"And to answer your next question," Marylou continued with a smile, "yes, a thief could easily sell one of her pictures. Very few dealers would immediately identify her work unless it was signed. Again, a reputable one would check the register of stolen art but, as I said, not everybody does."

"Hmm, very interesting." Molly was deep in thought. "So, Sol displayed all his priceless paintings, the Degas, Corot, Matisse, and others in his reception rooms while he kept two pictures of far less value in his study, where he spent most of his time, according to Daphne. He must have been particularly attached to these two pictures, maybe for sentimental reasons. Apparently the naked woman over the mantel reminded him of Daphne. And the Bay of St. Tropez in Blanche Camus' painting was perhaps the view they enjoyed from their room when they honeymooned there, who knows? I only wish I had looked at the pictures more closely when I still had the chance. Now… we might never see them again."

CHAPTER 10

"You know, of course, why I am here, ladies and gentle-men. The Palm Beach police were called in yesterday to deal with a robbery. Then they found a body." The man paused briefly to let the enormity of this statement register.

"My name is Gonzalez and I am an FBI Special Agent, attached to our field office in Miami. I am now in charge of the investigation. We presume that somehow these two crimes are linked, but at present we are still pretty much in the dark."

Special Agent in Charge Gonzalez was addressing Daphne Caplan and her friends the following morning. After an earlier phone call to explain that he had taken over from Detective Middleton, he had arrived promptly at Mon Trésor and was now applying himself with due formality to this latest case. Or cases.

Emilio Gonzalez, a second generation Colombian, was a large man in his forties who, were it not for his inquisitive eyes, might have passed for an undertaker on account of his dark suits and mournful expression. He was tall for a Latino but fulfilled all the other stereotypes: thick raven hair, moustache and dark eyes. Quietly unassuming, with a solid build and slow, deliber-ate gestures, he was capable of giving the impression that he wasn't hugely bright. But the success of his career proved oth-erwise. His quietness was his method. He preferred listening to talking, and was a relentless collector of details, fitting facts together like the pieces of a puzzle.

"As I said, it is more than likely that the theft and murder are connected and therefore I would like to check the alibi of everybody who was around on the evening before last. With the exception of Mrs. Caplan — that is, Mrs. Sarah Caplan — Mrs. Miller and Mr. Harding, everybody's fingerprints have been found in the study."

Again he paused, giving his audience the chance to take in this latest piece of news.

"I understand that the study in this house is not a public room in general use like the sitting room and the dining room. Everything in it had been left just as it was in Mr. Caplan's days and, if I may say so, it was kept a little bit like a shrine to him." Gonzalez gave a sidelong glace to Daphne, who nodded in agreement.

"The door was always closed and it would have been unusual for any guest to enter the room, at least without asking for permission. Is that right?"

Again, Daphne nodded.

"I would of course expect to find Mrs. Daphne Caplan's fingerprints and those of the housekeeper" — he looked at these people as he named them — "and of Ewa, who, I understand, occasionally took over the dusting from Betty and put flowers into the room. But I would like to hear why" — he scrutinized at a piece of paper in his hand — "Mr. Paul Caplan, Miss Deborah Ferolito and Miss Lucinda Carter went into the study. And when.

"However," he interrupted himself, "let me first ask you a few more general questions about the burglary. Mrs. Caplan, would you be so kind to tell me what happened on that day? Did you go out? When did your guests arrive? And did you have any other visitors?"

"That's quite easy" said Daphne. "In the morning I had a chat with Betty, and after we decided on our menu for the evening I drove to Publix to do some shopping. I came back in time for lunch, which I had with Lucinda and Ewa. Lucinda had only just got up and she then spent the rest of the day at the pool. Ewa had insisted on polishing some of our silver in the morning and she kept to her room after lunch, probably studying."

She looked over to the girl, who signaled her agreement.

"At four a visitor joined me for a cup of tea," she continued. "Simon White is our attorney and he is also a friend of the family. He popped in at my request because I wanted to discuss a legal matter with him."

She hesitated for a moment.

"Well, I might as well tell you. It concerned my will. Although I hope to be around for a long time yet, I make it a point to remember all my good friends in my will and occasionally I ask Simon to add a codicil. For instance if I want to leave a sum of money or some other gift to a friend or – and this happens too – to cut someone out."

Molly had placed herself in such a way that she could see the faces of most people assembled in Daphne's house that day. She noticed that Sarah and Paul exchanged a fleeting glance when Daphne mentioned the will.

"Simon was still here when Paul and Sarah arrived. They know each other and we all sat together for a while until Simon left and then Paul and Sarah went to their room to unpack. About an hour later Deborah and the other guests arrived. That's all, I think."

"Thank you, Mrs. Caplan. I will try to see Mr. White later today. Meanwhile would you mind telling me a little bit about your will – and perhaps that of your late husband? I don't want to appear intrusive but it might prove helpful."

"I don't mind at all; it's more or less common knowledge anyway. My husband left the bulk of his fortune to a foundation that uses the income — which is to say, the interest — for a number of designated charities. I kept our private real estate, jewelry, some of the paintings and enough to be comfortably well off for the rest of my life. For Paul, his only child, Sol had set up a trust fund about ten years ago which pays him and Sarah a monthly stipend.

"After my death all the major paintings will go to the Metropolitan Museum in New York where they will be kept together and displayed in a special Sol Caplan room. That's fixed. But everything else that Sol left me, I can do with as I wish. To tell you the truth I change my mind about that from time to time. That's why poor Simon has to appear intermittently to adjust the paperwork." Daphne smiled.

"Did you just talk to Mr. White or were there any papers, notes or anything like that?" the agent wanted to know.

"Well, let me think," answered Daphne slowly." I had made some notes which I read to Simon and he wrote things down in a little notebook of his. When we finished I put my papers into a drawer of Sol's desk."

"Thank you, Mrs. Caplan. Maybe I could now interview Ms. Ferolito, Mr. Caplan and Lucinda separately in the dining room. You know this, of course, but it is a fact that most burglars receive help from someone inside the house."

He raised his hands when he noticed the shock on several faces and anticipated protest.

"Of course I am not saying that this was the case here; but it is something we'll have to consider. Then there is the matter of the alarm, which remains a mystery."

The agent frowned and looked at his well-worn but prodigiously polished black lace-up shoes as if appealing for an answer.

"Betty, the housekeeper, comes usually to the house before anyone is up. She lives in a separate cottage, behind the garage, the servants' quarters, if you like. She lets herself in with a key and then switches the alarm off by punching in certain numbers. I imagine you all know this?"

Gonzalez looked around to make sure everybody was paying full attention to his words.

"On the morning after the pictures disappeared, Betty found the alarm active and untouched, not that she suspected anything. As always she switched it off. If the alarm is active a siren sounds when the doors or windows on the ground floor are opened: that's the doors between the hall and reception rooms including the study, and all the doors leading into the garden. The system for the entrance door is slightly different. If you come in from outside and the alarm is active, it emits a noise and you have thrity seconds to deactivate it. When the pictures were removed from the house the alarm must have been switched off. It was not forcefully immobilized, we would have seen that.

"No… someone, who knew the combination, de-activated it temporarily. But who was that someone?" Gonzalez let the last question hang in the air. He did not expect an answer.

The first to face an interview with Agent Gonzalez was Deborah Ferolito, Sol Caplan's secretary and confidante for many years. Sol had appreciated her intelligence and loyalty. She in turn had been devoted to him — and with such intensity that it was thought to be a reason why she had never married, although there was no suggestion that their relationship had ever strayed from the professional to the personal. It was simply that she found fulfillment in her work, and that Sol's larger-than-life personality had dwarfed any man she came into contact with.

Deborah had stopped working for Sol when he retired to Florida, where he employed a part-time secretary locally. The Caplans had occasionally met up with Deborah, either in New York or Palm Beach where, as they insisted, she was always welcome. Her present visit had been a surprise but a pleasant one.

These were the facts Gonzalez had found out since taking over the case. And as he now sat opposite her, he could see that Deborah Ferolito was a serious, thoughtful woman, soberly dressed in a dark, fitted suit and white shirt as though still working in an office. She was tall, over-slim with short dark hair, almost certainly dyed but expertly so. She was Daphne's age but looked older, maybe because she lacked the other woman's outgoing, easy manner.

Deborah kept her hands firmly clasped in her lap while she sat opposite the agent in Daphne's dining room turned interrogation center. She was pale and sat bolt upright. Everything about her spoke of nervous tension, even alarm.

"Miss Ferolito, I have to ask you this. On the night of the theft…did you go into the study?"

The woman opened her mouth, took a deep breath and then spoke, at first so softly that her voice was almost a whisper but slowly gaining in strength.

"I would not lie to the police or to you, the FBI. Yes, I went to the study in the middle of the night after everybody had gone to sleep. Daphne had given us the alarm code, just in case we felt like going downstairs during the night or into the garden. When all was quiet I slipped out of bed, went downstairs and disengaged the alarm."

She hesitated for a moment but Gonzalez urged her on. "Why was that? What were you doing in there?"

"I… I looked for a piece of paper, a letter. I knew that Sol had kept a lot of letters, important ones. He once showed me a secret compartment in his desk where he had hidden some important business papers and a couple of love letters from Daphne and a sweet little note from Paul when he was a little boy. I wanted to check whether he had kept a letter I once wrote to him. Agent Gonzalez, it is not easy to talk about this and I am deeply ashamed about what I am telling you now."

Gonzalez could see how uncomfortable the woman opposite him was. He felt sorry for her but was determined to hear her out. He gave her an encouraging nod and she continued.

"Many years ago I made a complete fool of myself. It was in New York. Sol and I had completed a complicated and highly lucrative deal. We were both euphoric and celebrated with champagne. And I got carried away and fancied myself in love with him." She shook her head. "I find it hard to believe now but I actually wrote to Sol, declaring my love for him. He chose to ignore the whole thing and we never talked about it. Sometimes it seemed to me that I had dreamed this whole incident. But I knew I had written that wretched letter and I was too embarrassed to ask him to return it to me. When he died I was terrified that he might have kept it and Daphne would find it. That's why I came here – to retrieve and destroy the letter.

"I pretended to be ill as an excuse to stay the night. Then, as I said, I slipped into the study and opened the desk-compartment. But my letter was not in it. I am now sure that Sol destroyed it. I just went back to bed, after turning the alarm back on again. The whole incident took less than ten minutes. Oh, and I am sure the paintings were still there when I went in. I didn't exactly look at them but I know I would have noticed if they had been missing."

Deborah sat back, closing her eyes briefly, and a small smile played now around her lips. She seemed relieved to have parted with her guilty secret and her body began to relax.

"Thank you, Miss Ferolito. What you told me I will treat in confidence. I'm sure you will find some sort of satisfactory explanation for Mrs. Caplan as to why you entered the study."

She nodded and gave him a weak smile as she got up to leave the room.

****

Paul Caplan was a picture of guilt, the words Bad Conscience almost written on his face. Gonzalez could barely suppress a smile as he sat opposite the younger man who had replaced Deborah Ferolito in the witness chair and watched him repeatedly pull at his shirt collar as though fighting for air. Paul cleared his throat noisily, wiped his forehead, and played with his wedding ring, all the time studiously avoiding the agent's eyes.

Gonzalez gave him a moment to compose himself and kept silent. Then without preamble, he threw down the question, "Why did you go into the library that night?"

These few words, spoken in a conversationally non-threatening way, had dramatic consequences. Caplan all but jumped out of his chair. He changed color and Gonzalez was afraid for a moment that he was suffering some sort of collapse.

Finally, in a voice that was almost inaudible, he spoke.

"I…we…it wasn't planned…we just, well, we thought…. You see, there was the question of Daphne's will. Damn it, I know we get a tidy sum every month but it's never enough. We always seem to spend so much more than we have. Eternal cash flow problem. I've always got on well with old Daphne and had hoped she would leave me some of her loot after her death. It is after all my Dad's money and I am his only son. Well, Sarah is certainly counting on some extra income.

94

"Anyway, when we arrived Daphne had obviously just discussed her will with that lawyer, White. I saw her put her notes into Dad's desk. During the rest of the day there was no chance to snoop around in the study but Sarah was determined to find out what Daphne's plans were. She woke me in the middle of the night and asked me to go down and look. Daphne had given us the number for the alarm, so that was easy enough to turn off. I found the damned paper in the desk but it only mentioned some funds for the Historical Society of Palm Beach and that money should be made available for Lucinda's college fees. Nothing about the jewelry or the pictures or anything like that."

Paul took a sip of water from the glass he had brought with him. Little pearls of sweat stood on his forehead, and when he took his glasses off, Gonzalez noticed that his eyes were red.

"I put the paper back where I had found it, closed the door, re-set the alarm and went back to sleep. That's all. Not very noble but hardly a crime. No need to tell Daphne, Mr. Gonzalez, don't you think?"

"No need at all," said the agent with a pleasant smile. "I imagine you wife will confirm all this?"

"Oh absolutely," answered Caplan with obvious relief in his voice.

Gonzalez now asked whether Paul or his wife, as far as he knew, had ever heard of or met a man called Yuri/John Poliakoff, and the answer was an unequivocal "no." Then he spread some photos out on the dining table. They had been taken by the police photographer of the dead man. The main damage had been inflicted to the back of his head but fortunately there was no need to show that. The face had also received a blow, but his features were quite visible. "They have done a fine job cleaning him up for his portrait," thought Gonzalez.

Paul was obviously reluctant to look at the dead man, but he knew there was no escaping it. He steadied himself sufficiently to look almost calmly at one picture after another and then, unhesitatingly, shook his head.

It was lunchtime by now and although Daphne invited Agent Gonzalez to join them, he excused himself. He had to return to his temporary office in town and proposed to come back for further questioning around three in the afternoon.

CHAPTER 11

Once again the inhabitants of Mon Trésor assembled for lunch on the terrace. Today Betty had rustled up some cold gazpacho, a chicken salad and grilled vegetables. Daphne began to wonder when she would ever have her privacy back. It seemed a long time since she had the house to herself and could indulge in a solitary meal if she felt like it. This man from the FBI would return later today and no doubt tomorrow. Maybe even the day after.

The meal was delicious and those responsible, Betty and Ewa, received lavish praise. Lucinda's T-shirt message of the day — Where have all the virgins gone? — might normally have started some amusing banter, but today nobody felt like laughing. The young girl was even quieter than in the past. The events of the last days had clearly left their mark on her. But she was more attentive and made a visible effort to join into the general conversation, for which Daphne gave her full marks.

When her guests relaxed over coffee and tea, the hostess excused herself and made her way to her bedroom for a rest. Paul and Sarah withdrew to their own room. Ewa disappeared to the kitchen. Lucinda put on her bikini and told everybody that she could be found at the pool. Scott, who had shown laudable foresight by bringing his own trunks, announced that he would join her after he had made sure that his aunt was comfortably resting in the shade.

Uncharacteristically silent, Molly contemplated the beauty of this south Florida garden, designed with taste and maintained with expertise. The pool was discreetly hidden behind a tall hedge to the right. The hedge in turn was partly screened by white flowering hibiscus trees. In front of the terrace, where they had enjoyed lunch under the shade of an awning, the lawn rolled gently down to the water's edge. And the rose garden, surrounded and intersected by dwarf hedges in the English manner, was barely visible to the left.

In the past she had spent many hours in this garden, admiring the beauty of the roses, their fragrance, and their very survival in this less than suitable tropical climate. Daphne, determined and well-informed, had taught Desmond the gardener how to feed, water and shelter her precious plants. They were a good team, the elegant Englishwoman and the stocky bearded South African, united by their love for nature. Daphne had been keen to offer him the use of a cottage at the back of the property, although he had chosen to remain in Wellington where he had a far larger, ranch-like house and children in school.

The grounds were generally well stocked with flowering trees and palms but the view to the inlet in front of the property had been left uninterrupted on purpose. Having direct access to the water, whether the lake or the ocean, was what every Palm Beacher dreamed of. It was also why the prices of such properties ensured that they remained, for any but the seriously rich, a dream.

Looking out from the Caplans' home over the inlet you could enjoy an endless parade of boats. From dinghies to water taxis and occasionally large black painted military naval vessels, they all passed by as if they were part of an elaborate theatrical scenery, moved along by invisible stage hands. Twice a day The Palm Beach Princess, a gambling cruiser, made her way out into open waters where the passengers could play their games without legal concern.

Then there was little Peanut Island on the left, closest to the north end of Palm Beach. No peanut, other than of the salted, pre-packed variety, had ever been found on this man-made pile of sand; it took its name from the peanut factory that should have been built there but never was. One thing that did get built, though, was a nuclear bunker, installed for President Kennedy when he used his parents' ocean front mansion as an informal winter White House. Sol Caplan, who had always enjoyed telling his guests about the bunker, never failed to mention that however wretched it would be to stay there in post-nuclear confinement, there had been, at Kennedy's insistence, one concession to good living: a luxuriously appointed king-sized bed.

On the east side, to the right, densely built high rises had completely obliterated the charm of Singer Island and served as a constant reminder for Palm Beachers of the dangers to their own island if they ever relaxed their vigilance against unscrupulous developers.

Molly, protected by sun block and a wide-brimmed straw hat which she had borrowed from Daphne, watched Deborah, who had taken refuge at an informal seating area complete with chaise lounges near the water's edge. Slowly and leaning heavily on her cane, she made her way over to the other woman.

"Hello", she announced her arrival, not wanting to startle Deborah who seemed absorbed by a book she held in her hand. "Please don't let me disturb you. I'll just sit here quietly and enjoy the view."

"That's quite all right," replied Deborah, closing her book. "I can't concentrate anyway with all that's going on."

"May I see what you are reading?" asked Molly, leaning forward to glance at the cover.

"It's the life of Queen Elizabeth...." Deborah began.

But before she could finish, Molly had interrupted her enthusiastically. "How fascinating. I am very keen on biographies, myself. I loved Laurence Leamer's books on the Kennedy men and women, so very a propos here in Palm Beach. Have you read them?" Deborah shook her head, smiling. She was quite happy to let Mrs. Miller rattle on and merely listen. It was really rather soothing.

"I'm a great supporter of the British royal family, despite all the negative publicity they have received since Diana died, poor thing! I don't think Charles was a good husband to her. But someone who never puts her foot wrong is the queen. It must be quite discouraging for Charles to know that he'll never reach the stature and popularity of his mother." Molly, who followed news, stories and rumors about European royalty with determination, would have happily continued in this vein had Deborah not corrected her.

"My book is actually about Elizabeth I, the Tudor queen."

Molly was thwarted but not beaten.

"Oh, I see. Well, that's another admirable woman, a great politician, diplomat, and military leader." Contrary to her nephew's impression that she only indulged in Regency romances, she did sometimes tackle more demanding books as well and enjoyed discussing them.

"Not just a Tudor queen, of course, but a virgin queen. Can you imagine how much pressure there must have been on her to marry, five hundred years ago?"

Deborah laughed. "In some ways she was a role model for me, although I wasn't aware of it at the time. She was the first truly emancipated woman and succeeded against all odds."

With a look Molly encouraged Deborah to tell her more.

"Well, she came from what you'd call these days a pretty dysfunctional family: her mother executed by her father, and four step-mothers in rapid succession before she was 13. How healthy is that for a child? But on the plus side, she was given a first rate education that was rare for a girl, and she clearly inherited her mother's ambition and her father's willpower. In so many ways she was ahead of her time. All her life she conducted that Virgin Queen business like a highly successful PR campaign. She just had an instinct for successful self-promotion."

Deborah was now in full flow, "I talked to Daphne about her yesterday and she made a very astute comment. She knows about British history and politics of course, and she saw a direct line stretching from Queen Boadicea to Elizabeth 1 and Margaret Thatcher, all of them formidable female leaders. Warrior queens, if you like."

"Hmm," mused Molly. "When you look at it that way, we in the United States are really quite backwards. Women in public life, Eleanor Roosevelt apart, are only just coming into their own with prominent figures like Hillary Clinton and Condoleezza Rice."

"I grant you, women are striding ahead, but having the same rights still doesn't mean being given the same chances. And until recently so many people had these fixed ideas about the role of women. Take me for an example. My family was horrified when I started working for Sol. I think they hoped it would only be for a few years, until I did the right thing – in their eyes, which was to settle down with a nice young man and have 2.5 children."

She smiled.

"But that didn't happen because I never met a man who appealed to me and was free. I don't know exactly why it is, but there are always more women around than men. I read recently that a single woman over thirty in New York is more likely to be hit by a meteor than find a husband. Well, that's anecdotal but not too far off the mark.

"Another reason why I remained single was, I guess, because I became involved in the all-demanding world of commerce and high finance, so much so that it made domesticity boring by comparison. I saw too many of my contemporaries stuck in loveless marriages. And when the children had flown the nest and they tried to start their own life it was too late. They had lost their skills or their confidence, usually both, and were reduced to living their lives through their children and grand-children. Thank God I recognized that early enough. I may have felt sometimes a little short-changed on romance, but looking back I wouldn't have it any different."

Molly appeared thoughtful. She understood what the other woman tried to say even though it failed to correspond with her own experiences and expectations. A career would have held little attractions for her. A loving marriage was all she ever aspired to and her life with Jim had fulfilled her complete-ly. How lucky that women nowadays could decide for themselves which way to go.

At that moment Molly felt, more than she heard or saw, the advancing presence of a man behind her. One of the uniformed policemen approached with a request from Special Agent Gonzalez to join him in the dining room. It seemed hardly possible that their two-hour lunch break was already over, but when Molly checked she found out that it was well after three.

CHAPTER 12

Gonzalez, while he waited for Molly, had ample time to look around the Caplan home.

It was impressive, no doubt, with its fine furniture, expensive-looking fabrics and, of course, the paintings. But he realized that the pleasing result was more than down to money. Even his untrained (except in police work) eye could tell that everything was chosen and arranged with taste.

And yet, given the choice, he would forego all this splendor without a second thought in favor of the home near Fort Lauderdale that he shared with the companion of his life, the admirable Teresa. Gonzalez had seen enough residences like the Caplan House in Palm Beach or similar ones in Miami and Naples. He didn't like vast expanses of marble, he didn't care for antiques, and he was not interested in fine art.

Teresa, though, was different. Once she heard about this latest case and that he was back in Palm Beach she would cross-examine him as usual about the lifestyle of the rich and mighty. He would be well advised, if he valued his peace, to make some mental notes about the dress sense of the people he was dealing with – not to mention the design and contents of their houses. Teresa was bound to ask.

Gonzalez loved his wife and he loved his domestic peace even more. But Teresa had been distant recently. Was it her job, in an accountant's practice? Was it her health? Maybe they were just too busy these days, he conjectured. Maybe they should take some time off, soon, and go away. The two of them. A second honeymoon. Somewhere romantic.

When Molly finally appeared, Gonzalez went through some prepared formalities – to which she listened silently, smiling encouragement. "Mrs. Miller, normally I would not discuss a case with anyone other than professional colleagues; but in view of our previous cooperation I think I can make an exception."

Molly looked duly gratified, and he continued: "As it happens, this latest crime again involves some of your friends, and I imagine you can tell me more about them in an hour than I could find out in a week. I interrogated Deborah Ferolito this morning. What do you know about her? To put it bluntly: Did she have an affair with Sol Caplan?"

Molly answered without hesitation. "Absolutely not, I would bet my life on it. Coincidentally I had a long chat with Deborah this morning. She is not one of these women who take a job to fill in time until Mister Wonderful turns up. I am not an expert on these matters but she seems to me a truly emancipated, or maybe I should say liberated, woman.

"She found a great job, she was successful and satisfied with her life. I guess it's human nature to look occasionally longingly to the other side where the grass seems greener. But I think she always came to the conclusion that her turf suited her just fine.

"Also, believe me, and this is more my area of expertise, I recognize a potential marriage wrecker when I see one and Deborah was not like that. No, the Caplan marriage was rock solid. Deborah was not more than a trusted and efficient assistant to Sol. Of course it may be feasible that she had a crush on her boss. I have no proof for that but I am an old romantic. Or should I say cynic?"

"All right, that was more or less my impression. Next: Is she short of money?"

"That I don't know. I'm certain that Sol left her reasonably well provided for - he was such a generous man. But I heard that she plays the stock market; and unless you're lucky as well as smart in that game, you're liable to lose your shirt before you can say Standard and Poor's."

Gonzalez raised an amused eyebrow at this unexpected display of familiarity with the world of finance. "Well, let me recapitulate my investigations so far. Anyone in the house that night knew the alarm combination and could, in theory, have helped an accomplice to enter the house and steal the pictures. Right?"

Molly nodded. "And the fact that some left their finger-prints in the library does not make them particularly suspicious. Isn't that what you are going to say? Anyone involved in the robbery would have made sure NOT to leave any marks."

"Spot on, Mrs. Miller, as always," said Gonzalez, brightening visibly. His face in repose could normally be described as melancholic. Today, however, he looked animated, almost excited. And at Molly's suggestion he gave her a lively, if abbreviated account of his interviews with Paul and Deborah.

Molly listened in silence and only shook her head disapprovingly when Gonzalez talked about the letter. "Did you speak to Betty, Ewa and Lucinda as well?" she wanted to know.

"Yes, I did," he replied. "Betty Jackson has been with the Caplans for three years. She came highly recommended and Mrs. Caplan is very pleased with her. She has excellent references. The only small problem with her is that, prior to her present job, there is a gap of nearly five years in her résumé which she can't adequately account for. She claims to have spent these years with her married brother in Canada. We'll have to check on that.

"Lucinda is not really a suspect. She only just finished school and arrived recently for a visit in Palm Beach. She had no problem explaining her fingerprints. She said she left them during the day when she sometimes goes through the study into the garden. For instance, when Mrs. Caplan has guests, Lucinda avoids the drawing room and the terrace and goes through the library to the pool. I can accept that.

"But then we come to Ewa, who may be the most important piece in our jigsaw puzzle. We showed her a photograph of the murdered man this morning and she identified him as her cousin. The poor girl was in a terrible state. The cousin was quite badly disfigured from the blows to his head but he had been sufficiently cleaned to make him recognizable. She told you yesterday, and me today, that she expected Yuri, or John, to visit her on the night of his murder but that he never turned up. A message she had left on his cell phone was never answered. By the way, he did not have a phone on him when we found him, though he did have a wallet with his driver's license and quite a bit of money. He certainly was not robbed, at least not of cash. It seems the murderer wanted something else from him, and it may be connected with Yuri's comment to Ewa that he wanted to entrust some object – or some information - to her keeping. Unfortunately, he didn't say what it was.

"Ewa is a bright young lady who came four weeks ago from Poland and will stay with Mrs. Caplan until August when she starts on her Ph.D. in Neurolinguistics at Columbia University in New York. Her English is excellent. She is quite shy and likes to make herself useful. Mrs. Caplan is very fond of her. Ewa is the only person in the house who had any connection with the murder victim."

"So, little Ewa is at present your prime suspect?" asked Molly, concerned.

"Yes, we know that Yuri Poliakoff came to see his cousin that night. But he fits into the picture in yet another way. Excuse the pun. He worked in the art world, for the Morales Auction Gallery in Miami. That hardly looks coincidental, does it?"

"But Ewa was with Daphne and the other guests all the time?"

"Only until about ten-thirty. After that we only know about her what she tells us. Don't forget that the murder did take place sometime between 10 pm and midnight."

Molly thought about this for a moment: "The two cousins had not known each other very long, I believe?"

"That's right. When Ewa left Warsaw her parents gave her a telephone number for some relations in America and somehow she tracked Yuri down. She went three times to Miami to meet him. According to her, Yuri was bright, clever and successful. She told me that he went to college where he majored in French literature. He jobbed around for a while until he seemed to have found his niche in the art trade, starting at the bottom – as a porter – but soon working his way up to join the sales staff. Recently he was attached to the jewelry department. Apparently he had a good eye for quality and made some money buying and selling for himself."

"Which is not illegal, so long as you respect the guidelines set by your employer."

"Correct, and I am not saying he did anything wrong. In fact nobody has a bad word to say about him. But one might suspect that he got excited when he found out that his cousin Ewa was living in the house of the great art collector Sol Caplan. He could have organized the theft, with Ewa's help. This is a possible scenario. Then he fell out with his accomplice, whoever that was, they had a fight and Yuri was killed."

"And the accomplice, who killed Yuri, disappeared with the pictures. Well, Agent Gonzalez, that does sound reasonable," admitted Mrs. Miller. "I hate to think that Ewa had anything to do with the crime but the circumstances are too suspicious to be ignored."

"I will go to Miami tomorrow to talk to the people who knew Yuri. Especially at the auction house," said Gonzalez. "I'm afraid we haven't tracked down any real friends of his yet. He seems to have been a loner, someone who didn't much need the company of others. My colleagues have already been to his flat and started questioning his neighbors."

"Well," said Molly, "when you go to Miami you'll probably want to have a word with Daphne's art-dealer friend. I don't think you met Stephen van Dreesen. He advised Sol on his collection and he was actually the one who discovered the Reclining Nude, one of the two stolen paintings, many years ago. Recently he re-evaluated all the pictures after Sol's death. And he's quite a character. I'd love to know what you make of him."

CHAPTER 13

At 8:30 am the next morning Special Agent Emilio Gonzalez set off from his home in Plantation near Fort Lauderdale toward Miami, thirty miles away. The weather had changed from being unseasonably mild to the clammy heat that would last through the next few months until at least September. Thank God for air conditioning he thought as the system kicked in and immediately lowered the temperature in his black Cadillac.

He took Broward Boulevard and swung on the overpass east to join I-95. Traffic was heavy. I-95 was often called the most dangerous highway in the States and it was easy to understand why: the eight high-speed lanes were used by a lot of old people (typical Florida), and recent immigrants (not always the most skillful drivers) as well as trucks. Like everybody else Gonzalez settled on a speed of just over seventy which seemed to be accepted by the law.

He passed the airport at Fort Lauderdale and continued south at a steady pace, allowing the hum of the air conditioning to relax him into a contemplative mood as he let the morning pass through his mind.

Teresa still wasn't her usual self. Last night he had tried to interest her in his new case and mentioned the big houses, the paintings, the fashionable clothes – as far as he could remember, and the rest he made up. But Teresa had remained quiet, listening politely but without engaging. This morning she had not even bothered to join him for breakfast but had stayed in bed, making excuses about not feeling well.

This was unexpected. Gonzalez and his wife had been married for twelve years and known one another for three before that. Teresa was sensible, loyal: good at the house and good at her work in an accountant's office. Granted, she was no Latin firecracker, either in looks or temperament, but that suited Emilio just fine. He liked her generous, steady nature, her dependability, her clear-headed resistance to Latino flights of fancy. Maybe she had just become bored being married to him. He knew that his career made him a reasonably good catch, but he was under no illusion about his desirability in the looks and charm department.

But then — no, there had to be some other explanation. Most likely she'd been dealing with some complicated bankruptcy case or similarly trying work. Gonzalez admired all "number crunchers" as he thought of people who could not just read a balance sheet but see beauty in their logic. Long lines of figures made his eyes these days glaze over, while they lit a sparkle in Teresa's.

The irony was that he himself had started out on his career path with accounting. That's how he had met Teresa, at the University of Miami, where he was two years her senior. But unlike her, Gonzalez never felt passionate about his chosen profession. His parents had talked him into it, and it seemed an opportune way to get on in the world. So he took his degree and did an adequate job in a big advertising company in Miami. After a few years he came across an article in the Financial Times about the FBI. He learned that the Bureau was trying to recruit candidates from racial minorities in their drive for diversity.

When he further discovered that a degree in accounting — or law, languages, computer science — was an ideal preparation to become a Special Agent, he applied almost instantly. To his amazement, he was hired and received his eighteen weeks of training at the FBI Academy in Quantico, VA.

Although daily life as a special agent never resembled the glamorous world of James Bond, Gonzalez had never for an instant regretted his career change. He was proud to serve his country, he got along with his colleagues, and valued the change and challenges each new case presented.

Gonzalez passed now the first signs for Miami, and was briefly tempted to follow the signs east at Exit 4 to the beaches. But he kept his foot firmly on the gas until he came to Exit 10, where he left the Interstate.

Driving came easily to him and his thoughts drifted again once he knew he was on the right road. He forced himself to prepare mentally for the two interviews he had planned. Although Gonzalez came to Miami quite frequently – his field office was located in North Miami Beach – he didn't like the city. As someone who looked Latin and spoke fluent Spanish he should have felt at home there. After all, Miami had become over the years an outpost of Cuba and the Caribbean as well as South and Central America. Spanish was now the dominant language.

But it reminded him too much of the environment he had fought so hard to escape: the cramped living conditions, the wild armies of children, the grown men sitting around idly, drinking and cracking jokes in Spanish while their women went out to earn money cleaning houses.

For all his strong black hair, his drooping moustache and brown skin, Gonzalez felt like an average, white, middle-class American, enjoying baseball and barbecue and living in a solid, prosperous suburb. Teresa, whose family came from Ecuador, had stronger links with her background. She tended to speak Spanish in the house and was constantly in touch with her family in Tampa.

Gonzalez slowed down to read the street signs. He had a rough idea where he was going – the antiques area just off Biscayne Boulevard — but the one-way system threw him and he had to circumnavigate an extra block before he arrived at East 41st Street, location of the Morales Auction House. By sheer good luck he found a meter and pulled some quarters from his pocket. He was happy to leave his car for a while. A look at his watch confirmed that he was early. The auction house wouldn't open for another fifteen minutes and Gonzalez decided to pick up a coffee on the way. No matter how hot it was, he needed his skinny latte every few hours.

Killing time and sipping from a paper cup, Gonzalez ambled past the galleries that lined this street, examining the artwork in their windows. Once or twice he actually went inside to ask the price of an item that had caught his eye. This was a new experience, a foray into unknown worlds. As far as he remembered he had never bought a piece of furniture in his life, still less a painting or a sculpture. He had lived in rental housing after leaving university; and when he married and bought the house in Plantation, Teresa had dealt with all that. Her taste ran to solid, heavy, functional furnishings and large, conventional oil paintings of still-lifes, flowers and landscapes, none of them with great claims to artistic merit. The home was well equipped and comfortable but that was it.

With time still left, Gonzalez was in no rush and enjoying this small art tour more than he would have thought possible, justifying it to himself as research. He came to the conclusion after a while that in this new world of fine art more was less and less was more. He smiled as the idea unfolded in his mind and made a mental effort to explain it, first to himself and later to Teresa in a way that she would understand.

Every time he spotted an item of furniture richly inlaid, generously curved and with plenty of gleaming brass about it ('ormolu' the professionals called it), it was not as expensive as he had expected. When he enquired about a plain piece with simple lines and no brass, the quoted price usually took his breath away.

The other rule seemed to be that shops filled to bursting with goods for sale tended to charge less than dealers who presented only one choice item in the window and demanded a king's ransom for it. Maybe he could persuade Teresa one day to come here with him and browse.

Gonzalez decided with a look at his watch that his research had to end and he turned back to the entrance of the Morales Gallery. None of the big auction houses, like Sotheby's and Christie's, were represented in Miami, which was surprising when you considered how much art, antiques and jewelry changed hands here, and how much money was around — not least from the stream of rich Latinos who came here in search of better investments than their own country's economy could offer. Alfredo Morales had discovered this niche business some 15 years ago; and from humble beginnings he had built up his auction house into a good-sized company with a large turnover and satisfactory profits.

Outside the double doors a billboard announced that furniture auctions took place on every first and third Monday; pictures were sold every first and third Wednesday; china, glass and silver every second and fourth Monday; and jewelry plus objets de vertu (whatever that was) once a month, every first Friday.

All around him people went about their way, walking in and out, some carrying big plastic bags with Morales printed in black letters on an orange base. The entrance hall was spacious, a little scruffy, with a large desk on the left where a bored young woman flicked through a magazine. On the right were some hardback chairs and tables with old auction catalogues on them.

Gonzalez approached the girl at the desk. "Is Edward Ritchie in? I have to speak to him."

As usual in these circumstances he made no move to show his FBI identification, preferring to retain his anonymity for as long as possible.

The girl gave him a contemptuous glance. He clearly didn't fall into her favored category of wealthy customers.

"Turn right after the glass door, last on your left, and you'll find him." Having exhausted herself with so much helpful information she ended the conversation by returning to her magazine.

Ed Ritchie, when Gonzalez found him, was a lean man of average height with a narrow face and a shock of black hair that belied his age — which was probably late fifties.

He was half-hidden behind a desk piled high with books, papers, boxes, a computer, and other modern office kit: a printer and a fax machine. Looking around, Gonzalez decided that this was probably the messiest room he had ever encountered. One whole corner area was taken up by a massive, old-fashioned safe. Apart from a single, spare chair there was no further furniture in the room. All the available floor space was taken up by unstable looking towers comprising more books, catalogues and files.

"Yes?" was all the man said as he peered over his glasses at the visitor.

This time Gonzalez did produce his FBI badge, prompting a sudden change of attitude. Ritchie introduced himself and asked his visitor to take a seat.

"I want to speak to you about Yuri Poliakoff. I gather he was your assistant?"

Before Ritchie could say anything he continued: "You know that he is dead?"

Ritchie looked suddenly pale and nodded. "Yeah, hell, what a shock! The police came yesterday and told us. What a terrible thing to happen! We are all still reeling from the news. They interrogated everybody who had dealings with him, and that's actually most of the people who work here. We are quite a small company." He stopped for a moment and continued hesitatingly. "They said he was killed. Do you know yet who did it? I just hope you'll find the bastard. I am glad we still have capital punishment here in Florida. The only way to deal with swine like that."

Gonzalez shook his head – partly in answer to Ritchie's question, partly in response to Ritchie's views on crime and punishment. Although he knew all the arguments in favor of the death penalty, shared as they were by most of his colleagues, he remained strongly opposed. But this was neither the place nor the time for discussions of that sort, and he forced himself to concentrate on the case again.

"I am afraid it's far too early to say. I am sorry if you have to answer questions that you were already asked yesterday. Please bear with me. First of all: How long has Mr. Poliakoff been working here?"

Ritchie stretched himself, folded his arms behind his back and looked up at the ceiling as if waiting for inspiration. "Well, Yuri has been working here for four or five years. He doesn't have the theoretical knowledge, he is not an art historian but he is a clever chap. He started off as a porter, kept his eyes open, learned on the job and as time passed he took on more and more responsibilities until he was taken on, about a year ago, in the sales team. He first did a stint with pictures and has been assisting me for the last five months with jewelry and objets de vertu."

Noticing Gonzalez' quizzically raised eyebrows, he added: "That's valuable, usually small items. Faberge eggs, snuff boxes, stuff like that."

"When did you last see him?"

"Three days ago. We were preparing for an auction next week, looking at items, valuing them and doing some research, normal stuff. We both left the office at the usual time, about six o'clock. I can't remember who packed up first."

"Did Poliakoff tell you what plans he had for the evening?"

"No, I haven't the slightest idea. Although we worked together we didn't socialize much. We hardly ever talked about private matters. But that doesn't mean I wished the poor man any ill. We were on perfectly friendly terms. I liked him a lot. I asked him a few times to have a drink with me but he always declined. He kept pretty much to himself."

"Did you know anything about Mr. Poliakoff's family? Did he mention, for instance, that a cousin of his was staying at present in Palm Beach, at the house of Mrs. Sol Caplan, the art collector?"

"He mentioned his cousin. A girl with an accent, I assume it was Polish, rang once or twice for him but she never introduced herself and I had no idea where she was staying." Ritchie answered all questions willingly enough.

"Do you know whether he had any enemies? Did he seem anxious to you? Perhaps depressed?"

122

"As I said before, Yuri wasn't a man with an easy temper, an outspoken guy. Even if he had been in some sort of trouble he wouldn't have talked about it, at least not with me."

"Would you mind telling me a little about your work and the auction house? Luckily my wife is not particularly interested in jewelry and so I know very little about it."

Ritchie gave a smile as was expected of him and sat back in his seat.

"To put it very simply: in the jewelry business it's all about diamonds. They are rare, they are pricey and they are, as the saying goes, a girl's best friend."

"Go on," Gonzalez prompted.

"What do you want to know? The price depends on size, quality and color. They are measured by weight: the carat. The diamonds you see in the windows of high street shops are usually between one, or even half, and ten carat. When you talk priceless jewels the weight goes up to six or seven hundred carats and the price to millions."

"Fascinating," murmured Gonzalez. "And what about fakes?"

Ritchie shot him a quick glance. "That's not something we like talking about. There are several man-made copies, like zirconium and monazite: cheap to buy and indistinguishable to the naked eye but obviously not the real thing. Experts can't be fooled: everybody in the trade has a tester. Wait." He scrambled around on his desk, opened drawers and finally picked up a little metal instrument shaped like a thick pencil. "When you touch a diamond with this it will beep and flash. Hold it on to a man-made stone and nothing happens."

"OK, I understand all that. Tell me a little more about what you and your colleagues do here! Is there a big market for second-hand jewelry?" Gonzalez, with his enquiring mind, was genuinely interested in what he learned today. "I hope I am not keeping you from your work?" he added politely.

Ed Ritchie made an expansive gesture with his arm. "To hell with the work. Let's talk. There isn't much to do this early in the day and we have no sale this week anyway. OK, the answer to your question is: huge. Consider the people who sell. High street shops pay damn all if you go to them with a ring or broach, however good the piece may be. They can buy gems at competitive rates and they're more interested in selling their own stuff. Most good jewelers don't have a huge turnover; maybe they do in terms of value but not quantity. So, at best our customers would get a fair price for the stones, if they are good. The workmanship is immaterial."

"I see," commented Gonzalez. "So, if I ever should find myself in the enviable position of having a surplus of jewelry to offload, I will come to you and not go to a shop. But what about the buyers?"

"There are different sorts of people who buy from us. Some are dealers, because they may be commissioned to look for a specific piece. Then there are the secondhand jewelers: some of them specialize, say, in art nouveau pieces or work from the fifties and sixties. And then we get young couples, looking for an engagement ring or a birthday present. People who appreciate or even collect gems come on a regular basis to see what's coming in and there is always the chance to find a bargain. The same people might come back after a while and sell. So, you see it's an interesting business and lucrative too, otherwise Mr. Morales wouldn't bother."

Ritchie looked at his hands that he held meticulously folded in front of him on his desk. Gonzalez noted that they were strong and well shaped.

"It may interest you that our auction house has a lot of South and Central American clients, as you would expect, I suppose. Miami is now predominantly Latin and the Morales family came originally from Ecuador. The majority of our customers are Spanish speakers."

"Habla Español?" asked Gonzalez with a smile.

Ritchie looked up and laughed. "Sorry, that I understand but I am one of the few people working here who doesn't speak Spanish."

"To go back to Mr. Poliakoff, I'm not clear about the job he did here."

"Like I say, he was my assistant. He had learned about art and antiques in the years he had worked at Morales. He had no specific training but he was intelligent and picked up things as he went along. I trained him, if you like. Of course I was responsible for the valuations but he put the catalogues together from what I told him. He seemed to like what he was doing, there were no problems."

"And you never met any of his friends? Overheard his phone calls?"

Ritchie shook his head. "I never met anybody. Of course there were telephone calls for him but I think nearly always in connection with business. Don't forget that he would have used his cell phone for private calls. He once mentioned that there was a group of guys, I think at least they were all guys, who met sometimes for a beer. But I don't know any more. You would have to ask around."

Gonzalez nodded. He had already decided on that. He had probably found out as much as he could have hoped for. There was just one last thing. He was already half way at the door when he turned around and asked: "Not that it's important, but do you have any practical training? Do you know how to make jewelry?"

Ritchie looked up in surprise. "As a matter of fact, I did do a basic course, some years ago. It's always useful to be familiar with the technical aspect of the stuff you handle. But I am certainly not a jewelry maker."

Gonzalez nodded. He had been there for almost an hour, so he thanked Ritchie for his time and left the auction house.

The agent returned to his car and took the Airport Expressway west. On Lejeune he turned south and was ten minutes later in Coral Gables, a fashionable part of Miami with elegant homes, expensive shops and a few well-established art galleries. Much of Miami consisted of undistinguished rows of suburban houses, one or two stories high, with pleasant enough tropical gardens but bland and without architectural merit. This historic part was different. There were still old Spanish-looking houses, the wide streets shaded under the canopies of trees that had been planted a long time ago. You could find open-air cafes, well patronized at this hour before the midday heat would drive the customers inside where they were safe from the strong sun but exposed to the merciless blast of icy air conditioning.

Why was it, Gonzalez often asked himself, that we Americans don't handle our air conditioning with reason? Restaurants were usually kept far too cold and before he ventured to a movie theatre he stocked up with at least two woolen sweaters to keep his body temperature above freezing point.

With interest Gonzalez let the Spanish street names roll down his tongue: Seville, Mallorca, Alhambra Circle, Salvador Street. Because he suspected that his next visit might take up a little more time, he searched for and found a parking garage. A few minutes walk brought him to Ponce de Leon Avenue and before long he saw the name Van Dreesen Art Gallery on an awning to his right. There were only two paintings in the window, obviously by the same artist: large pale seascapes where vast sways of gray-blue water merged indistinguishably with the horizon. On one a dark smudge might be a boat. The other one showed a faint flat line possibly indicating some distant land.

Gonzalez pushed the door open and found a bespectacled young man looking at him from behind a desk at the far end of the gallery. When the visitor entered, he rose and asked politely if he could help. He was a tall young man with curly blond hair, fashionably dressed in chinos, a navy blazer and a striped shirt, open at the neck. There was something nervous and scholarly about him: the way he kept pushing his glasses back with his left hand.

Gonzalez identified himself and asked to see Mr. van Dreesen. "I am so sorry", the young man explained. "He won't be coming back to the gallery today. I am his assistant, my name is Gus Reuben. Can I help at all?"

"Maybe," replied Gonzalez. "Are you familiar with the Caplan collection? Your boss may have told you that two pictures were stolen. I have just been put in charge of the investigation."

"Oh yes, indeed. We have talked about it," cut in Reuben eagerly. "Why don't you sit down?" He pointed to the visitor's chair opposite his desk.

"You may also have heard that a man has been murdered on the property, around the same time as the robbery took place. We suspect there is a connection but have no proof yet. That's why I talk to as many people as possible."

Gus Reuben expressed his horror about the death, which was no news to him. He explained that his boss had called him this morning to tell him, before the papers carried the story.

Gonzalez settled himself more comfortably and began asking his questions. He was immediately informed that neither Reuben nor Mr. van Dreesen had ever met or even heard of Yuri or John Poliakoff. They were of course familiar with the Morales

Auction House, but he at least not from personal experience. Reputable dealers, Reuben explained sniffily, didn't buy and certainly wouldn't sell their stock there. In his opinion it was a gathering place for small dealers and private customers, often Latinos, who needed a quick sale.

Gonzalez asked the young man to tell him a little about himself. Reuben gave him a surprised look but came up with the desired information. He had a doctorate in fine art and restoration from McGill University; and having slaved as an overworked and underpaid sub-curator at the Montreal City Museum for a while he had joined the van Dreesen gallery five years ago. He had found the job through an advertisement in "Art International" and declared himself perfectly happy in his present position. He was familiar with the Caplan collection. He had met the Caplans on several occasions and had, together with van Dreesen, undertaken the revaluation of the paintings after Sol's death. In fact, several of the pictures had on that occasion been cleaned and some even restored, in a minor way, by him personally.

"How long did that take?" Gonzalez wanted to know.

"Oh, we were there for about three days. We stayed at the Chesterfield Hotel. I cleaned most of the paintings on the spot and we took three of them back to Miami for about a week. They were, let me think, a Dali, a Dufy and a little Corot. I have a small studio here," he pointed to the back, "where I can do limited restoration work."

"How did you get into the house when you were in Palm Beach? Were you given a key? Did they tell you how to switch the alarm on and off?"

"Oh no," answered Reuben almost horrified. "None of that. We were let in and out by the housekeeper or Mrs. Caplan herself."

"Were you aware of the alarm system in the house?"

"Yes, of course. The whole of the ground floor is fitted with infrared motion detectors. When the beam it emits is interrupted, the alarm goes off. This happens, for instance, when someone opens a door or a window. The major paintings are all individually secured. When that system is activated you cannot even touch any of the pictures because an alarm goes off instantly, in the house and at the police station. Furthermore, the paintings are screwed to the wall. It's not a question of lifting them off the hook and running away with them."

He paused for a second. "I guess, a ruthless or desperate thief could cut them out of their frame..." He shook himself and forced a faint smile. "That's not something I would like even to think about."

"So, even if someone managed to get into the house, it would have been difficult to remove one of those pictures and get away?"

"Not just difficult, practically impossible," Reuben confirmed. "This sort of sophisticated security cannot be disengaged, even by an expert criminal. At least I have never heard it could."

"How about the two pictures in the library?"

"The Friesz and the Blanche Camus? Well, that's a different matter. If you immobilized the house alarm you could just walk out with those two. In fact, we valued the Friesz at about $ 150 000 in the present market and suggested to Mrs. Caplan that it should be better protected. Whether she followed our advice, I don't know."

"No, she didn't. That's why the thief was successful. I expect the pictures are by now on the list of stolen art work that the police circulate. You presumably know about that list?"

"Of course. As it happens, I checked it on my computer

this morning, and the Caplan pictures were even accurately described."

"Do you think they will ever turn up?"

"Hard to say. If the thief is a fool, he will try to offload them, for a modest amount, right away and be in danger of discovery. If he is clever, he will lie low for a while and then secure a deal. Of course this could have been a commission job, or a robbery for ransom. But I believe no demand has been made and frankly, the pictures are not quite in the league for serious ransom money."

"You don't happen to know why Mr. Caplan kept just these two pictures in his study, do you?"

Dr. Reuben shook his head. "I am afraid what goes on in the minds of rich collectors is usually a mystery to us regular humans."

The agent rose and shook the younger man's hand. "Thank you for your help. We may have to come back but that's all for today."

He was almost at the door when he turned back and asked in a friendly voice: "This is just a formality, but would you mind telling me what you did on the night of the robbery, when the man was killed?"

"Not at all, Mr. Gonzalez, I expected the question. Mr. van Dreesen and I both attended an art show on South Beach. It was a big affair and lasted well until midnight. We met friends and colleagues who, I am sure, would have no problem remembering us. I am happy to give you the address."

"Thank you, Dr. Reuben, that's all."

He had barely left the gallery, when Gus Reuben picked up the telephone and began dialing.

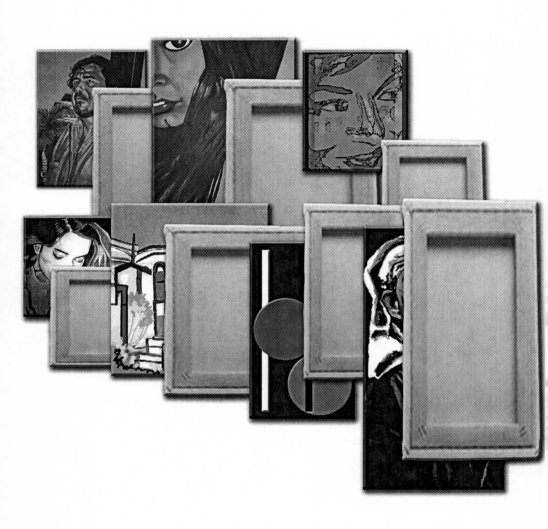

132

CHAPTER 14

Palm Beachers had woken to yet another flawless May day, but for Molly it came close to the limits of what she could tolerate in comfort. A few degrees up the scale and she would suffer. As it was, she flashed a happy smile at Scott on entering the kitchen where he was already settled in his usual place. He raised his head from behind the newspaper, planted a theatrical kiss on the cheek offered to him, and launched into the first high-energy discussion of the day.

Molly was beginning to get used to this lively routine first thing in the morning. Her normal habits were more tranquil, living on her own for so long with no one but Manolita for company until lunch time. But Scott was used to early starts and noisy, quick-fire banter with his office colleagues that he seemed to want to re-enact in Molly's kitchen. Daily.

He now waved the local newspaper in his hand and stared with a grin at his aunt. "I'm having hysterics over your Shiny Sheet again. Do you know that they are in open warfare with another venerable newssheet, the highly esteemed Palm Beach Today?"

Molly responded noncommittally.

"Then let me tell you. These two worthy publications, easily read and digested, spend time, effort and no doubt money fighting each other. And why? I mean it's just comic-strip stuff about Palm Beach high life. Pictures of peculiar-looking people with bizarre names in weird clothes. Where's the world news? The economic and political analysis? It doesn't happen. All you get is photos of Ms. Ylang Ylang de Vere Klopstock at the Broken Heart Foundation ball. I just love it. To think that people here get their take on world affairs exclusively from local papers gives me palpitations."

He looked at his aunt who affected token indignation alongside the amusement she found hard to mask.

"Slow down, darling," she countered. "I know what you mean, but what you don't realize is that the Shiny Sheet is not just a newspaper. It's a treasured institution and it belongs to Palm Beach like The Breakers or Addison Mizner or our clubs. If you want world news and hard-hitting editorials, read some other paper. We love our Shiny Sheet for what it is. During the season, some people here cannot have their morning coffee without it. They call each other up to discuss the pictures and whether Robert Janjigian and Shannon Donnelly described their parties accurately. Serious socialites have the paper sent to them in their summer resorts: Newport, Long Island, Nantucket, you name it. And that's despite the fact that no major parties take place outside the season."

Molly noticed that Scott was anxious to press his case again but she was prepared to defend her ground.

"I fully realize that we are not at the cutting edge of social awareness on this island, and I know the world out there is a pretty sordid place. There's not much we Palm Beachers can do to change it, but we do take an interest. We give huge amounts of money to charity and we do vote. By the way, it may surprise you to know that Palm Beach County has a Democratic majority. OK, generally we have an easy, gilded life here, but you're not going to make me feel guilty about that. Guilt is not conducive to positive action. Awareness is. I've had my share of ups and downs and I try to be a good citizen and true to my friends and family. So allow me some credit, please, for my life, however small, sheltered and cosseted it may be."

"Oh, I'm sorry Aunt Moll", said Scott, more calm now than his previous tirade suggested. "I don't know why I get so hot under the collar about a place that is, in physical terms, so very beautiful and where people, it has to be said, go out of their way to befriend you. Palm Beach is OK. It's just – well, maybe you have to be over fifty to value the general atmosphere of leisure, waste and luxury."

"Look, I grant you that the island is not your average American town. But being unique it deserves to be valued and preserved. Yes, a lot of people here are what you young people call filthy rich, but don't forget that they give staggering amounts of money to charity."

"Which is of course a means to social advancement," said Scott dryly. "But what can you expect from a town where people die and leave trust funds in their wills for their dogs?"

At this point Molly laughed and clapped her hands to signal End of Combat. "That's enough. I never argue on an empty stomach. Have another croissant!"

After ten minutes aunt and nephew had finished breakfast and, with it, their perusal of the morning papers which Molly folded neatly.

"Scottie, I hope you haven't cancelled your golf game? There is no need, you know. Life goes on, even after murder."

Scott admitted that his plans were unchanged.

"Splendid. I hope you have enough time to drop me off at Daphne's house first?"

"Sure, if you can be ready in 15 minutes?"

"No problem. If you want to get the car, I'll be downstairs shortly. And don't worry about me later, Daphne promised to give me a lift home."

****

At Mon Trésor life had returned to something like normality. Deborah Ferolito, still in enforced exile from home, was writing letters in her room. She would be returning tomorrow to her friend's house in Hobe Sound, even though she had been forbidden to leave Florida for the time being. When Molly arrived, Paul and Sarah were just setting off in their hired car to go downtown. Sarah had made appointments with a hairdresser and a masseuse. An appearance as elaborate as hers demanded regular and thorough maintenance.

They had plans to lunch out with friends and were not expected back until later in the day. Daphne was delighted – not only that they were gone but that they actually had friends to go to. And besides, she had her own plans for the morning. She was on her way, together with Molly, to visit a neighbor.

The Contessa was a woman of indeterminate age, certainly over seventy, with a severely tightened white face under unnaturally black hair pulled back into a chignon. Her lips and long nails were like drops of blood, her wrists, fingers, neck and earlobes weighed down with jewelry too large and too colorful for Northern taste. She had grown up at the Royal Court of Morocco. Her father had been a friend and adviser to the then king and her first language was French. Nobody remembered where and when she had acquired her aristocratic nickname but it had preceded her arrival in Florida. People who didn't know her well took it to be an allusion to her opulent life-style and social ambitions, but it stood in delicious contrast to her sometimes shockingly crude language.

At the appropriate age she had married a wealthy American and they lived on their own private island in the South Sea. By sheer coincidence they discovered that the well water they had always used not only tasted good but was also replete with beneficial minerals and trace elements. They bottled it, distributed and sold it; and soon half the western hemisphere was covered with pleasingly shaped plastic bottles containing, as the label said, Pure South Seas Island Water from the Crystal Cascades. Within not too many years their enterprise had turned them into billionaires.

When the husband died, the widow moved to Palm Beach where she expected to console herself with another man, ideally younger. But to her dismay she found there was a long waiting list for suitable consorts. When she met Charley she decided on the spot that she had to have him. He was a handsome fellow, some twenty years her junior: a great card and backgammon player, perma-tanned, gray-haired, charming and, though not rich, with a thoroughly attractive lifestyle. A short, long-forgotten marriage had provided him with two satisfactory children, both married. And now he was free to spend his days on boats and his evenings escorting any attractive woman in Palm Beach who showed interest in him.

Nadine, which was the Contessa's real name, found herself besotted; and it drove her into rages that he wasn't readily available. She showered him with Rolex watches and cashmere sweaters and made it quite clear that no price was too high if only he would move in. But while Charley was never one to miss out on an agreeable affair or turn down a diamond-studded watch, he had at the same time a healthy instinct for self-preservation and was not to be bullied. His horror of commitment and the experience of occasional jealous scenes with Nadine made him realize that life with her, however gilded, would be unbearable.

She tried every trick and inducement in the world but in the end had to accept defeat. A few months later her best friend, Georgette, told everybody — in strict confidence of course — that Nadine was a happy woman again thanks to the unspecified services rendered by her new, extremely handsome butler. With Charley out of reach, Gaston was the next best thing for the amorous widow: attractive, attentive, and always available.

The Contessa lived in a substantial mansion on one side of Daphne, between her and the public dock. She had designed the house herself, an opulent Moroccan fantasy surrounded by romantic courtyards, terraces and fountains. And the view they afforded of Daphne's own grounds suggested that she should be approached for information concerning the night of the double crime. After conferring with Molly, Daphne had called and made an appointment to visit this morning.

Now the two women stood outside the heavy iron gates: Molly leaning on her cane and Daphne pressing the door bell repeatedly. At last a heavily accented voice replied through the intercom and the gates swung open with majestic tardiness. The ladies staggered across thick gravel never intended to be walked on, least of all by invalids, but merely driven over. At the equally impressive glass front door they had to ring and wait again, until it was cautiously opened by a young, apparently foreign woman in a pretty pink uniform and frilly apron.

This pleasing picture was only spoiled by the heavy white sneakers she wore. Seeing them gave Molly a slight stab to the heart. She missed her own sneakers, her exercise, and its attendant satisfaction. She hated being forced to lumber around with a bandaged foot ensconced in a slipper.

Proofs that the maid was foreign were her black hair, an olive complexion and a sketchy command of English that required Daphne to explain, slowly and loudly, that she was expected at eleven o'clock, pointing to her wrist-watch. The girl looked at them doubtfully and then, deciding that their likelihood of being burglars or terrorists was negligible, opened the door wider and showed them in. In halting terms she explained that she would make inquiries and that they had to wait for her right there.

Molly looked around with unconcealed curiosity. Daphne, who had been to the house before, noticed and smiled. The entrance was an impressive double cube with a large chandelier hanging from a great height above. It was clearly Middle Eastern with its gleaming brass and multi-colored glass. The floor was solid marble, as was that of the next room, which opened out behind an arch, and of a further room behind it in the distance. Thick carpets broke the huge expanse of white. On the walls hung curious art works: mirrors in flamboyant frames and oil paintings of desert landscapes, men smoking the 'hubble-bubble,' and scantily-clad beauties flashing dark eyes at the viewer. The furniture included grand gilt consoles, hard-backed chairs with inlaid ivory, and other Eastern artifacts.

Before Molly could look further or had a chance to peep into the next room, the maid returned and beckoned them to follow her. They stepped through an arched doorway into the garden and walked along a path, graveled again but bordered by white shrubs emitting a heavenly fragrance, to a tent — if one could call this charming folly by such a prosaic name. The hexagonal little structure consisted of embroidered canvas pulled around a frame, leaving space for windows and a door. The ogee roof line was accentuated by a scalloped border which extended around the canopy over the open entrance.

Advancing, they heard some strange slapping noise accompanied by a spine-chilling screech. Molly and Daphne looked at each other in surprise.

They were invited to enter and, as they did so, faced an astonishing scene. In the middle of the room was a large, high bed, and on it a body completely covered by a thin white sheet except for the head. A uniformed attendant bent over the reclining figure and pressed his hands on her, massaging the concealed flesh by stroking, pushing and occasionally slapping through the fabric. One look explained the screech. In an elaborate cage a vicious-looking parrot gave the newcomers a noisy welcome, scratching and flapping in a way that sent feathers and bird food flying.

"Shush, be quiet," came the husky voice of what turned out to be their hostess, shrouded on the bed. "Please excuse Scheherazade, she doesn't like visitors." So much was clear.

Daphne introduced Molly and apologized for obviously having got the time wrong. "I thought we were supposed to meet at eleven, Nadine, we certainly don't want to upset your plans for the day."

"Rubbish," said Nadine. "I thought you were coming at twelve but I always get my timing in a muddle. If you like we can just talk while Laurence finishes his job. I need my massage at least every other day; I got used to it in Morocco and never needed to change my routine."

"Well, if you don't mind, we'll just ask you what we would like to know and be as quick as possible about it," said Daphne hurriedly. "You know what happened at my house, I suppose — the robbery and the death?" she asked.

"Damn nuisance," came the voice from the bed. "The bloody cops were here and asked me a million questions but I just said I had been smoking opium and was fast asleep all night from seven onwards." She chuckled. "They didn't like it but it's all they got out of me."

"But that's not true, I take it." Molly now took up the inquiry. "What exactly did you hear or see next door at Daphne's house two nights ago?"

"I never sleep before midnight and the opium smoking was just crap. At this time of the year I keep my windows open and because it's so devilish quiet here where we live, every passing car is a major event. One car passed my house at about ten, parked at the little dock and never left, at least I didn't hear it drive away. Another car drove up shortly after and stopped on the road, between Daphne's house and mine. This second car was probably bigger and newer, guessing from the sound the engine made. It drove off again after about ten or fifteen minutes. I thought the driver might just have collected something. Not a person though because I heard no voices at all. There may have been a third car but that was later and I'm not entirely sure. After midnight I closed my window wondering who in hell were all these people? Almost everyone round here has gone away for the summer so you kind of expect the place to be quiet as a morgue. But not that evening," she rattled on.

"Thank you, Nadine, you are a sharp observer," said Daphne with a meaningful look to Molly. "If there's nothing else, we should probably leave you alone now. You need your rest."

At that moment the masseur made an unwelcome movement and from the prostrate body came a screech not unlike those still issuing periodically from the repulsive parrot. The Contessa turned on her attendant and bellowed: "Leave us alone! Send Gaston!"

Molly and Daphne got up in an attempt to show that they were serious in their intention to leave but raising a languid hand the Contessa stopped them.

Within seconds, Gaston, the handsome butler, dressed in a most becoming uniform of tight white trousers and an emerald green fitted jacket with a Nehru collar, appeared at his mistress' side as if spirited there. At his heel followed a beautiful black spaniel, playfully jumping up at the man and barking. "Shut up, Duke!" roared the Contessa; and, turning to Gaston, she demanded: "Lift me up!"

He knew the routine. With a practiced movement Gaston raised the top of the massage bed to an angle that returned Nadine into a half-sitting position.

"Let's have a glass of champagne," she suggested to her guests.

"No, no, thank you dear," replied Daphne hurriedly, "but I would love it if you came over for lunch sometime next week."

"Absolutely. I know you have no butler, shall I bring Gaston?"

"No, please don't bother, we'll manage. I have Betty in the kitchen and a very nice girl to help her. I'll call you tomorrow."

Molly said a few appropriate words and together they left the massage tent. Expecting Gaston to see them out, Molly turned around at the entrance. Looking back, she saw that he was still attending to his duties at the bedside — where Nadine had taken his hand and directed it under the sheet that draped her naked body.

142

CHAPTER 15

Belle and Maxwell's was the latest 'hot' lunch place in Palm Beach, admittedly off the island, but such was the charm of the décor and the quality of the food that it hadn't taken long to become equally popular on both sides of the bridges. It was located on the east side of South Dixie Avenue, five minutes from the Southern Boulevard, in a nondescript little square surrounded by antique shops. This was where Daphne proposed to take her friend Molly since their neighborhood visit had been a short one and they both expressed a keen interest in lunch. The little encounter with the Contessa and her household had highly amused Daphne, and her euphoric spirit led her to expand her largesse further.

"Why don't we take the girls with us? Ewa and Lucinda haven't had a very nice time lately. They'll love this place; everybody does. Luckily it's still early enough to get a table for four. What do you think?"

Molly, who always liked the company of young people, thought this an admirable idea and once the girls were tracked down – Ewa from the garden where she helped Desmond deadhead the roses, and Lucinda cruelly driven out of bed – it took them only fifteen minutes before they headed south in Daphne's smart BMW convertible. Molly had never been a great fan of open-topped cars. They spoiled your hairdo and made you swallow too much dust for her taste, apart from putting the air conditioning out of work, but she would never have objected since she knew the girls were keen to 'feel the wind in their hair.' Mr. Miller had once on an ill-considered impulse bought his wife a beautiful Sebring convertible. Of course she had shown due pleasure and gratitude but, to tell the truth, in the seven years she owned the car, she had not once taken down the roof.

The girls hopped into the back and Daphne helped Molly get into the passenger seat not forgetting the cane. While Daphne installed herself behind the wheel, Molly pulled a little organza scarf out of her handbag which she carried with her just for such occasions. She draped it over her hair, knotted it under her chin and, thus prepared, managed to enjoy the drive to this new promising place.

Parking was no problem and a good table was instantly available. Belle and Maxwell's charmed because it was so non-American, not slick and streamlined but slightly chaotic and bohemian. Noisy, lively, cluttered, with furniture that looked as if someone had collected the contents of several attics – tables, high and low, hard chairs, armchairs, squashy sofas, rugs and cushions and all sorts of old fashioned ornaments, all cheerfully jumbled together. Apart from the welcoming ambiance, two things made the little restaurant irresistible: the charming young staff and the superb food. Today's special was spinach quiche with salad which they all opted for except for Ewa who chose a Cuban sandwich from the regular menu. They ordered raspberry tea.

Daphne looked around her with satisfaction. The gloom of the last two days had lifted. She and Molly told the girls about their visit to the Contessa, which made Ewa giggle. Lucinda glanced slightly self-consciously down her T-shirt where the message, spread in large letters over her chest, read: What are

146

you looking at? Daphne caught her eye and they both laughed. When Molly asked how many printed T-shirts Lucinda owned, the girl confessed that she had come to the end of her supply. Daphne promised to take her to Macy's in CityPlace where she was sure they could pick up a few new tops. Even Ewa had begun to address her appearance with small changes. The stiff little plaits had given way to a much more flattering ponytail and instead of her overall she wore white trousers and a shirt.

Daphne looked around to signal for the check when she noticed a young man sitting by himself in a corner, absorbed in a book that he had propped up in front of him. "Carlito," she called out spontaneously. The young man lifted his head and, when he recognized Daphne, he jumped up and came over to their table. She invited him to pull up a chair and join them for a moment. "This is Carlos Brutta who owns a divine antique shop around the corner," she said. Then she introduced her friends. Carlos, who had a mop of brown curls and a most attractive smile, declared himself delighted to encounter such charming company. He wanted to know all about the young girls and gladly offered himself as an escort in case they needed 'male protection' as he called it. Daphne thought this was a brilliant idea. She was an inveterate match maker and in her mind's eye saw already visions of two happy couples, Ewa and Scott, Lucinda and Carlos, walking into the sunset together.

Carlos pretended to be utterly shocked that the girls had not experienced the local nightlife so far. He claimed to be the greatest living authority on discos and nightclubs between Miami and Vero Beach with South Beach as his favorite research ground. "Daphne, may I borrow the young ladies some time and show them Miami? Lucinda cannot possibly leave Florida without having been to Opium and the Red Bar. I am an excellent guide and totally trustworthy," he said with a look of exaggerated innocence. Molly thought he was utterly delightful and when they left she asked him for his telephone number because she wanted him to meet Scott. Daphne suggested that he should come over to her house one evening soon when they could make further plans.

She noticed that Ewa, although polite as always, looked suddenly troubled and seemed preoccupied on their way home. As soon as they had dropped Molly off and reached Mon Trésor, Ewa asked whether she could speak to Daphne for a moment.

"When we met your friend, in the restaurant," she said," something came back into my mind. You know, Mr. Gonzalez mentioned that he cannot find any friends of Yuri's to ask them about him. Well, I remember something. Once, when I was in Miami, Yuri talked about place where he sometimes meets some friends, where they 'hang out' as he called it. It is Red Bar. The name stuck in my mind because I first thought, wow, is that a political meeting place? But it has nothing to do with politics. Yuri said, red is just color of walls and everything. I wanted him to show me this place and he promised to do it, next time. I don't know whether this is useful, what do you think?"

Daphne put her arm around the girl. "I am sure it is useful and I am very glad you told me. I think I'll call Agent Gonzalez right away and tell him what you said to me."

****

A few hours later, at seven o'clock in the evening, Agent Gonzalez was on his way back to Miami. That afternoon he had received two very interesting telephone calls. The first one had come from Molly Miller. She had told him about her visit to the Contessa and the new information about the traffic near her house on the night in question. "I am sorry, Agent Gonzalez, that the woman lied to your men. I am sure what she said today is the truth."

Gonzalez gritted his teeth. He was simply furious, with the Contessa for her willful concealment and with his agents that they been duped. Thank God that he had had the foresight to involve Molly Miller in the case and she had, once again, come up with the goods.

The second caller had been Daphne Caplan. What she had told him was of sufficient interest for him to follow up the lead immediately. He felt it best to go to the Red Bar himself and see what he could find out.

Traffic was not bad at this hour. It was still light and because he didn't need to concentrate too much on his driving, his thoughts drifted back to his domestic life, yet again.

Between Daphne Caplan's call and his start for Miami there had not been enough time to go home, as much as he would have loved to shower and change. He was not a vain man but even he felt embarrassed when he noticed how wrinkled his black suit looked. His shirt was not much better because he had not found a clean, ironed one in the morning. What was the matter with Teresa? She barely cooked these days. When he came home, half starved, he would just find a salad and maybe a sandwich waiting for him or he was told where he should look in the ice box and what he could expect to find. This had never happened before in all the years of their marriage.

Things would have to change. Maybe he should phone her mother? No, not that. If Teresa found out she would be furious. And besides, it might bring his mother-in-law from Tampa to their house in Plantation, undoubtedly for several days, and that was a prospect he did not relish. He just had to talk to

Teresa. The problem was that he hated confrontations; he had too many of those in his professional life. And, he had to admit, Teresa was a skilled debater. Somehow she always emerged victorious in their arguments, not that they had many. It was best to wait and see. Patience was what he needed. Yes, he decided to let things be for another week or so and then he could still take the necessary steps – whatever they might be.

It was almost nine by the time Gonzalez parked the car in downtown Miami, because he had stopped on his way to get a sandwich. Another sandwich – they seemed to be becoming his staple diet. The telephone directory had given him the address and he had found it without a problem: The Red Bar and Gallery on SW 10th Street.

Before he could open the door he heard a loud beat and a probably black voice ranting in a self-important monotone street argot. Although he could not claim to have his finger on the pulse of contemporary pop music, even Gonzalez recognized the music as rap. Once inside it became clear that the bar did justice to its name. The soaring high walls were painted bright red and covered tightly with pictures, of different styles, techniques and no doubt different artists. He would find out later that they were all for sale. Young painters could bring their work and, as long as the owner liked it, he hung it up and tried to sell it at a good price for the artist. No wonder this place had appealed to Yuri with his interest in art, thought the agent.

The room was quite dark but once his eyes had adjusted, Gonzalez saw a long bar on his right with two men sitting at it and several small tables with an odd assortment of comfortable-looking chairs, all red, on his left. He chose a bar stool near the entrance. A young man in white rolled-up shirt sleeves asked him what he wanted and at his request served him a beer.

"Do you know a young guy called Yuri who came here occasionally? That's him." And he slid a photo of Poliakoff over the table. In the dead man's apartment they had found some photographs of him which they could now use instead of those taken at the crime scene. The waiter glanced briefly at the picture and shook his head. "I'm sorry I can't help you. I only started working here a few days ago. But why don't you ask Court? He's the owner ... over there." And he pointed to another man behind the bar who had his back to them. When Gonzalez nodded he went over and came back with Court. "What can I do for you?" he asked. He was a young man in his thirties with pleasant, regular features who appeared effortlessly elegant in jeans and a pale blue shirt. He was very slim and so tall that he kept leaning forward, no doubt a longstanding habit to correspond with other people on their level. His hair was straight and so long that it fell constantly over his eyes. Every time that happened, he raked it back with the fingers of his right hand. While they talked, Gonzalez noticed that Court never stopped looking around him, but it wasn't done in a nervous, stealthy way. Checking that business ran smoothly was evidently second nature to him. Before Gonzalez asked him the same question he identified himself, adding that this was a routine inquiry and had nothing to do with the bar or any trouble.

Court took one look at the photo and smiled. "Sure, I know Yuri; he comes here occasionally. Nice chap, quiet, just has a beer or two, talks to some people he knows and goes home early. He likes to come on the second Wednesday of the month when the artists get together. He's in the trade, I think, and is always interested in the pictures. He even bought a couple, he has good taste."

"Do you know any more about him? Did he ever talk about his private life or his work?"

"No, not to me, but there's a chap called Brad who knows him better. Brad comes to us two or three times a week. He hasn't been for a day or two, so I think you have a good chance to see him later. He doesn't normally turn up until ten. Do you want to wait?"

Gonzalez nodded. With any luck Brad would appear and maybe he had something useful to say. He picked up a second beer and made his way slowly around the room looking at the pictures.

He was just contemplating an abstract that he could have sworn was hanging upside down when Court called him from the bar.

"Hello, Mr. Gonzalez, Brad's here."

The agent went over, shook the man's hand and told him who he was and what he wanted to know. Brad, a short man, rather stocky, with a ponytail and hands that seemed two sizes too large for his body, asked hesitatingly, "Yuri's not in trouble, is he?" Gonzalez felt that he should tell him the truth, since the newspapers were likely to carry the story tomorrow anyhow. They took their glasses and went to sit at a table. When Brad heard what had happened he was visibly shaken and pressed the agent for more details. Gonzalez told him what he thought was necessary and then carried on questioning him. Brad was an intelligent, well-spoken man and clearly had decided to help the police in any way he could.

He confirmed that Yuri was reticent although he had mentioned his new-found cousin. Brad hardly considered himself a friend but he had probably spent more time with Yuri in the bar than anybody else. No, there were no mutual friends, just a few acquaintances, not worth mentioning. As far as he knew Yuri had never fallen out with anybody. He was not a hot-headed sort of man, but rather quiet, a great reader.

Ah, his work, well, that was different. Yes, he enjoyed working at the gallery because he loved art but lately he had seemed less enthusiastic. Something had troubled him but he had never said what exactly it was. Somehow he had formed the opinion that Yuri didn't get on too well with his boss, the chap who ran the jewelry section, but nothing specific was ever mentioned.

The agent asked a few more questions but that was all Brad could come up with. Gonzalez thanked him for his trouble and said good bye. As he left the bar, that had now filled up considerably, his last impression was one of Brad looking miserably into his glass.

CHAPTER 16

Almost a week had gone by since the fatal night at Mon Trésor, and it became abundantly clear that the investigating forces, police and FBI were, as the saying goes, tapping in the dark. Mrs. Miller had given the unfortunate events much thought, often burning the midnight oil up to 11:30, well past the local witches' hour, pondering and discussing the matter.

Another perfect blue and golden day greeted her as she made her way into her kitchen, but a look at the thermometer confirmed that the temperature was rising alarmingly. So early in the morning, just after eight, it showed already 82 degrees. The race was on now between the oncoming summer heat and the healing forces of her foot. Giving the offending limb a reproachful look, Molly sat down at her breakfast table, for once beating Scott to it. Five minutes later favorite nephew appeared, tousle-haired and sleepy-looking but nonetheless ready for his intellectual sparring partner. He grabbed the Shiny Sheet, leaving Molly the comparatively harmless Palm Beach Post that gave little grist to his mill. It took him just a few minutes of reading, punctuated by wild groans and derisive chortles, before he put the paper down and confronted his aunt, who smiled at him angelically, having had sufficient time to prepare herself.

"Well, that's a nice little tussle you are having here over the Poinciana Plaza, isn't it? A perfectly good playhouse, built by an esteemed architect and loved as well as needed on the island is in danger of being pulled down by the owner of the plaza who proposes to replace it, and the equally delightful shopping center by – no price for guessing here – another rotten apartment block. You need more condos in Palm Beach like a hole in the head. There isn't enough parking anyway and if this Alice-in-Wonderland town continues, as seems likely, on its downward spiral, the entire island will be left without any regular commercial life to support it. Businesses will all move to West Palm and the island will turn into a Mickey Mouse theme park.

"When the Canadian whiz kids bought the shopping center, they agreed to keep the Playhouse as a theatre. Now they want to break their commitment by changing the zoning laws. Such duplicity is diabolical – all dictated by greed. And, as always in corporate America, some damned lawyers find a way to pervert the course of justice."

He picked up the paper once more, shaking it at Molly. "And I haven't even mentioned the best bit. In the meantime the Playhouse is boarded up so nobody can get in, and left to rot. Why don't you locals here do something drastic?"

"Like what, dear Scott?" asked Molly unperturbed.

"Oh I don't know, maybe you and your girlfriends could form a human chain around the playhouse, a virgin's watch or something but, of course, not until photographers are in place."

Molly couldn't suppress a giggle. "Nice try, Scott, but maybe we can come up with a better idea. In the meantime, I happen to know Mr. Paul Noble is doing a fine job of speaking out on behalf of our Playhouse. And, as you know, Jack McDonald is a terrific mayor. I have complete faith in him to guide Palm Beach in the right direction for us all. I'm hoping to have lunch with Jack next month. Do you have any other complaints … or, perhaps, constructive suggestions I can address to him on your behalf? He's quite a good listener."

"Actually, yes. I am all in favor of preserving good architecture. But if Palm Beach is to survive as an organic small town for real people rather than a lifeless anachronism, you cannot let it fossilize into a make-believe fairyland. If you do, the place will turn into just another variation on all the other country club developments. Instead of gates there are bridges as barriers to keep out the common and dangerous outside world. Islanders will pretend to live in a real town but will have to go to the mainland for any normal needs. All you can buy then in Palm Beach will be diamond-studded watches, cashmere sweaters, art and decorative home accessories. And. of course, don't forget, hugely overpriced bigger and bigger mansions on smaller and smaller lots.

"The next step could be a dress code, first voluntary and then, by and by, obligatory. All men wear nothing but shorts, chinos, button-down shirts and blazers; and never socks with their tasselled loafers. Women will by law have to don Lilly Pulitzer clothes, top to toe, oversized sunglasses and Nantucket baskets."

"Oh really, Scott? I admire your imagination." Her nephew had got so carried away with his visions for the future that Molly barely managed to get a word in. "Tell me more about these threats that loom large, so I can prepare myself."

"Well. Palm Beach is so exclusive that it has always aroused curiosity. But you dislike tourists. One idea is that you come to an arrangement with the state authorities to ban strangers totally from visiting the island. In return you will allow for carefully selected guided tours. Every so often someone is chosen (or will volunteer) to be on display for half a day or so. A busload of elite 'voyeurs' who pay exorbitantly for the privilege will be allowed to witness this family as they swim in their infinity pool on the edge of the ocean and eat lunch on their pristinely kept terrace surrounded by Mario Niviera-designed gardens. Then the visitors troupe off and the islanders are among themselves again."

"Well Scott, as long as I am not on display…By the way, what's wrong with Nantucket baskets?" Molly couldn't help teasing her nephew and tried to introduce a playful note.

"Nothing, dear aunt, I just wish that I sometimes met someone here who had a purpose in life and strong views other than self-serving conservatism. Someone who is still actually doing something other than filling his or her days with shopping, playing and exercising."

"You are harsh on us today, Scottie. I think I'll have to stop you here before I begin to develop a guilty conscience. Come back in thirty years time and you will see things in a different light, I promise you. But is there anything else you would like to change?"

"Yes indeed. If it were up to me I would force all your realtors to put up photographs of how they really look, now, not twenty years ago or airbrushed out of recognition."

Molly laughed. "You have a point there. But to come back to more mundane subjects: Do you remember that we have plans for this morning?"

He looked blank. "Really? Remind me."

"I have an appointment at Good Sam for 11 and you promised to take me."

"Well of course I will, Aunt Moll. That gives us another good hour to discuss local affairs and mores." To Molly's relief he said it with a grin and they both reached simultaneously for the coffee pot.

****

Her doctors were pleased with Molly's progress and expressed the hope that they might take the bandage off in another few days, which would enable her to walk more easily and even travel. This was good news indeed and Molly decided to set her plans for the return trip to Cleveland back into motion. Scott also was beginning to feel that his bank might not want to spare him any longer. All this sea air and golf was fine for a while but staying out of the strenuous competition in Manhattan's business world for too long was a dangerous game.

"Scott, I would be grateful if you could drop me off at the Colony Hotel. I'm meeting someone. You might want to go back to the golf course, I imagine," said Molly.

"Aha, a rendezvous, and I'm no longer needed. Well, young lady, I hope you know what you are doing. Shall I take you to the main entrance?"

"Actually, no, leave me at the coffee shop. And, don't worry, my 'date' will take me home."

Stopping at the desired spot Scott helped his aunt out of the car. He was too curious to drive off immediately and, as he looked around, he saw a man clearly waiting for Molly. He was half hidden behind a sunshade and Scott decided to wait. Then the man stepped forward to greet Molly, and Scott saw who he was – FBI Agent Gonzalez. Satisfied that his aunt was in good hands he drove off to collect his golf bag.

"I'm so glad you could make it, Mrs. Miller. What can I get you, would you like something to eat?"

"No, thank you, Agent Gonzalez. I'll just have a coffee. Is that what you're drinking?"

Gonzalez confirmed this, recommended his favorite, Skinny Latte, and, when Molly approved, went to the counter to fetch it.

They took their cups to an empty bench in the little garden between the hotel and the coffee shop with a fine view over South County Road toward Worth Avenue to one side and Golfview Road on the other side.

"Well, how far have you got?" Molly thought there was no point in beating about the bush. Obviously Gonzalez wanted to discuss the case and they might as well jump right in. She noticed that he seemed tired, friendly and polite as ever, but definitely out of sorts. Professional frustration, she assumed.

For once the agent's downtrodden expression fitted precisely his mood. "Blank, blank, blank," he confessed. "Neither the autopsy nor the forensic experts have uncovered any clues. We keep making inquiries, going with a fine comb through everybody's past but nothing turns up that brings us any closer to solving the case or maybe I should say cases. Needless to say the pictures haven't turned up. If anybody staying at the house that night was involved in the robbery, he or she would have had an accomplice. The most likely candidates, van Dreesen and his assistant, have cast-iron alibis."

"What about Betty, the housekeeper? Does she have any skeletons in the cupboard?"

"We checked up on her because we wanted to know whether there might be a connection with Reuben, who comes from Canada, but that seems unlikely. He hails from Montreal and she spent time in Toronto, admittedly under suspicious circumstances. She took a job there when she left Florida, about seven years ago and got herself into trouble when her employers reported to the police the disappearance of some of their jewelry and cash. Betty was accused and initially charged but nothing came of it for lack of proof.

"That must have given her a nasty shock. Either she couldn't find another job or she didn't have the courage to apply for one, but anyway she spent the next few years living with her brother and his family, helping out and taking the odd temporary position."

"So, as far as the robbery is concerned you'll have to wait until the paintings turn up somewhere, sometime and roll the case up from that end," mused Molly.

"Well, I hope not. There is still a lot we can do." The agent's voice was now firm again. He retained his mournful expression, so familiar to Molly, but his temporary despondency was all but vanished.

"We are circulating photographs and descriptions of the stolen paintings among all major galleries and dealers, not only in Florida, but also interstate. I will interrogate the neighbors again personally, particularly the Contessa."

He gave Molly a warm look. "Thank you for informing me of what she told you. She managed to pull the wool over my colleagues' eyes but I want to hear personally what she noticed that night, and she won't be able to fool me."

The agent spoke now with all the authority of a successful, energetic professional for whom failure is not an alternative.

"As for the murder, the only scrap of news we've come up with is, well, at this point no more than a rumor. We heard on the grapevine that the Morales Auction House isn't completely kosher. Apparently, irregularities have occurred in customer dealings. Whether these were oversights or attempted, maybe successful, frauds we don't know yet because nobody so far has come forward with an official complaint. Several of our agents are interviewing clients of Morales to get to the bottom of this. And, believe me, if there was foul play I'll find out about it.

This supports our idea that Yuri was bothered about his work. We know from two witnesses that he was upset about something. There is no suggestion from anyone that he had money problems or that a love affair had gone wrong. As far as we know he had no enemies. It is most likely that he had trouble with his job. If we are to believe Ewa, he had told her that he wanted to see her in Palm Beach to give her something for safe keeping. What was it?"

Molly, who observed him, smiled when she saw Gonalez pulling his moustache, an involuntary gesture she remembered well from their time together last year. This was a sign of full concentration. The agent was totally immersed in this latest case and made maximum use of the opportunity to run his thoughts by a like-minded spirit, as he thought of Molly Miller.

Gonzalez didn't wait for an answer but carried on, "A letter? An object? Maybe something valuable? A video or a tape that was incriminating someone? But let me just remind you: The purpose of his visit to the Caplans' house is uncorroborated; we only have Ewa's word for it. "

He paused for a moment and Molly knew what would come.

"Hell, I can't help feeling that the case hinges on that girl. For the moment she is still our prime suspect, if only from her relationship with the victim. Let's just assume the following: Ewa tells Yuri about the paintings and they plan to steal some of them. He turns up on the night with an accomplice. Ewa lets them in. The two men fall out over something, have a struggle and Yuri gets killed. – What do you think? It's a plausible scenario."

Molly shook her head with great conviction. "I know, I know. It could have happened like this and I have no better theory. But don't laugh when I say that my female intuition tells me, in no uncertain terms, that Ewa is not a criminal. That girl hasn't got a dishonest bone in her body."

"Okay," replied Gonzalez. "What have you got to offer? Who is your main suspect?"

"Nothing at present, just some vague ideas," Molly admitted reluctantly. "I've been thinking about Mr. Ritchie at the auction gallery. If Yuri's troubles were caused at work, who is more likely to be involved than his boss? Assuming that Ewa's story is true, Yuri wants to give her something important. Ritchie wants it back or wants to destroy it. How does he know Yuri will be outside Daphne's home in Palm Beach? Yuri would never have told him where he was going. That would have been counterproductive and dangerous for Ewa. Don't tell me Ritchie followed him! No way can you tail someone from Miami to Palm Beach and then to the quiet north end of an island where you hear a pin drop at night."

"The only person who might have something to say about that is Ewa. Shall we ask her again?"

"I think so. Will you allow me to speak to her? I think she trusts me and is more likely to help us if I'm the one to press for it."

Gonzalez nodded.

"If I find out anything useful at all I will call you instantly. Will you be at the police station here on the island?" asked Molly.

"Yes, for the rest of today."

Something else was on Molly's mind. "Tell me, Agent Gonzalez, is there any chance that I might be allowed to see Yuri's apartment? I assume you have not found anything of interest but I would really love to have a look for myself."

Gonzalez hesitated for a moment. He had the greatest respect for Mrs. Miller's intuition – her 'hunches' as she called them. But in this instant he could not imagine what yet another search of Yuri's apartment could reveal. They had gone through the place with a fine comb. He was certain that nothing had been overlooked.

But on reflection it was probably better to give in. "Mrs. Miller, you must understand that this visit you suggest, is, well, let's say, unusual. I'm afraid I cannot give you unsupervised access to the place. You'll have to put up with my company. If that's OK with you, we can go. When do you think?"

"How about tomorrow?" Molly answered quickly and with obvious relief.

"Okay with me. Shall we drive over together?"

"No thanks, Agent Gonzalez. My nephew is already booked to take me to Miami; I have some other things to do there as well. Why don't we just meet there at eleven, if that suits you? What's the address?"

They agreed on the time and Molly wrote down where Yuri had lived and how to get there. When Gonzalez offered to buy her another coffee, Molly declined but requested a lift home, which was gladly given.

****

"Ewa, can I talk to you for a moment or are you busy?" asked Molly. Barely twenty minutes after her meeting with the FBI Agent, she was on the telephone to Ewa.

"No, I am not busy, Mrs. Miller. What can I do for you?"

"Ewa, you said that you expected Yuri on the evening he died. He rang you earlier in the day and told you that he wanted to give you something. You tried to call him back but his cell phone was switched off. Listen, this is very important: Did you speak to him at all before he left the office?"

"No, I didn't. There was no answer."

"So, you did ring him at work?"

"Yes but, as I said, nobody picked up."

"Let me ask you again, Ewa. You didn't speak to Yuri or his boss, Ed Ritchie, after you received the message that Yuri wanted to come here to give you something. Is that right?"

"That is so. I only spoke to machine."

There was a momentary pause. Molly could barely suppress her excitement.

"You mean an answering machine? At the Auction House?"

"That's right. I wanted to confirm that I was expecting Yuri and I wasn't sure whether he had correct address because he had never been here. I rang office number I had for Yuri and when nobody picked up I just said: Yuri, this is Ewa, don't come tonight until late. And the address is 215 North Lake Road."

"Thank you, Ewa," said Molly happily. "That's great news."

****

Punctually at 9:30 am the next morning Molly and Scott set off for Miami. With the help of a good street map and thanks to Gonzalez's description, they found the little square without problem. Fairview House was a utilitarian looking seven-story block, probably built in the '80s, without aesthetic or artistic aspirations. They found Gonzalez already waiting for them in the parking lot, engaged in a telephone conversation. When he spotted them, he waved, ended his call and got out of his car. After a perfunctory greeting they entered the hall. The door was open and no doorman was visible. It wasn't that sort of building. They took the elevator up to the fifth floor, turned left and waited outside a door with the lettering 5C until Gonzalez unlocked the door.

The first thing to confront them was the stale hot air in the apartment. For a week nobody had opened the window, and the air conditioning, if it worked at all, was set far too high. It didn't take long to explore the place, with its small bedroom and moderately sized sitting room with an open-plan kitchen. It was more or less what Molly expected from the bachelor apartment of a poorly paid trainee auctioneer without a regular housekeeper. It was a place to live – that's the best that could be said – with cheap furniture. The fabrics, carpets and walls were all in various shades of dirty beige. The color of overcooked veal, an expression Molly had read once, came back to her. The whole place was remarkably untidy and, as was to be expected, very dusty by now. Every surface was cluttered with clothes, dishes, dirty glasses, books, and papers. In a corner a potted plant in need of water and dusting languished on a chest.

The only redeeming feature was the art work: an interesting modern sculpture on a glass dining table and several pictures, some hanging up, some leaning against the wall. There was a large, old-fashioned oil painting, a portrait of a lady, in a damaged gilt frame, which Molly recognized as English, some smallish watercolors and a few modern paintings, landscapes and abstracts in vibrant colors.

Books were everywhere: bursting out of the bookshelves, in and on tops of boxes, on and under the tables and in stacks on the floor. Scott picked up a few and pointed out to Molly that most of them seemed to be by French authors – novels, plays, short stories - some in the original language, some translated. Then there were books on art and antiques, jewelry, china, traveling, gardens. The spectrum was broad and the choice was testimony to the taste of an intelligent, well-educated person.

Gonzalez stood back and watched Molly as she walked around silently. He had, of course, seen it all before. She reminded him of a well-groomed Persian cat who steps gingerly through a new home, testing her surroundings scrupulously and suspiciously. Once Molly had familiarized herself with the place, she started to rifle through papers. She concentrated on anything work-related: old catalogues, brochures and trade magazines. She would pick one up, flick through it and then put it either aside or back with the others. Gonzalez was fascinated. He simply couldn't work out what she was looking for but didn't dare to interrupt her with his questions. From time to time he heard a faint hmm or aha but no explanation followed.

He pretended to carry out his own investigation, walking around, checking, but it was a half-hearted attempt to conceal his impatience. Every so often he would drift over and stand so close to Molly that he could look over her shoulder to see what she had in her hand. Her response would be either to put the paper down or to turn around so that Gonzalez ended up gazing up at her back.

Finally he couldn't stand it any longer. "If I knew what you are looking for I could help you," he said. He felt pleased with what he thought was a subtle hint to let her know that he would like to be kept informed of what was going on.

"If I were certain, I would tell you, Agent Gonzalez. At the moment I'll just see whether I come across something unusual." Molly's comment was accompanied by a stern look that in her youth had put many an over-ardent admirer in his place.

Gonzalez conceded defeat and gave vent to his frustration with just a heart-felt sigh, loud and reproachful. When this, as expected, elicited no response he finally sat down and pulled out some papers he had brought along in the expectation that he might have to fill in some time as productively as possible.

Scott had discovered some old copies of Playboy and, not knowing what to look for, decided to scrutinize them for want of better things to do.

When this had gone on for more than an hour, both men became impatient and looked more and more frequently over to Molly. She had now assembled a little pile of chosen booklets, which she leafed through more thoroughly.

At last she stretched out her hand to Scott and said: "Help me up, I think it's time to go."

"Well, were you successful?" asked Gonzalez with just a hint of sarcasm, looking up with relief from his own papers.

"Perhaps. May I take this magazine with me?" She held out a black and white brochure with the name Rapaport written in large letters over a wide red border on the top. Underneath it read: Diamond Report. "I think I should learn a little more about diamonds since this is what Yuri was working with." Gonzalez saw no problem with her request and took her arm when he noticed that she walked awkwardly despite her cane. Sitting and kneeling so long must have been very uncomfortable for her. All three left the apartment, left the building and got back into their two cars, going off into different directions.

"Where to next, darling aunt?" Scott wanted to know. "I'd better warn you. If we are spending as long at the next place, and especially if it's equally dusty, I shall require a good lunch and a very liquid one to boot," he said.

"Fair enough, I promise," said Molly. "If you'll take I-95 and get off at Exit 36, which will take us to Coral Gables, we'll get to the Auction House."

"Aha, super sleuth, I should have known we would eventually end up there. I am actually looking forward to seeing that place," said Scott pleasantly.

They found it without problems and were greeted by the receptionist whose bored face lit up noticeably when she saw Scott. Molly started her well-rehearsed sweet-old-lady act and had the girl in no time at all eating out of her hand. She got up willingly, went back to the office, then a store room, looked through some of the old catalogues on the front table and gave Molly readily all she had asked for and more. When they left, Molly well-satisfied, the receptionist looked wistfully after the retreating well-built figure of Scott.

Molly felt herself in need of some refreshment now and since they both were not familiar with Miami they followed the advice Daphne had given them and went in search of the Cheesecake Factory in Coconut Grove. As was to be expected they ate far too much – Sliders for Scott and an Oriental chicken salad for Molly. After some coffee and a shared ice cream they were ready to take up the trail again.

"And our next port of call," pronounced Molly, her spirits thoroughly revived," is Mr. Chen Kwa Dong's Gemporium, an 'Aladdin's cave of precious stones,' on Lincoln Road."

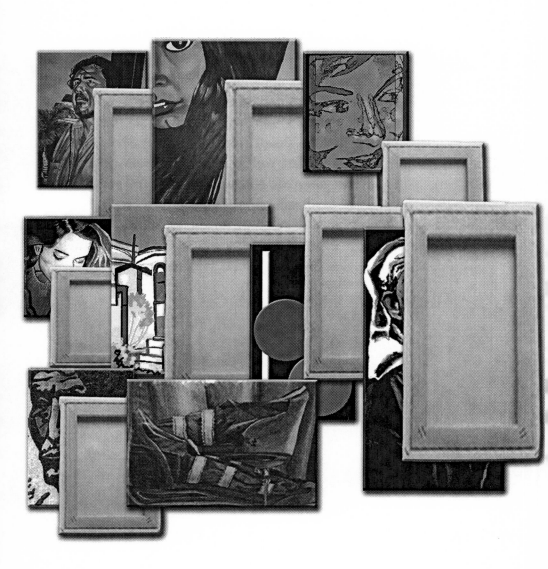

CHAPTER 17

"Agent Gonzalez, thank you for allowing me into Yuri's apartment yesterday. It was very helpful. I spent a little more time in Miami and I think the case is solved. The murder, that is. Is there any chance that you might get a warrant to search Mr. Edward Ritchie's office?"

Gonzalez almost choked on his latte. He had just arrived at his office, it was not even 8:30, and he didn't believe his ears.

"My dear Mrs. Miller," he exclaimed. "I hope you have good reasons, because if this is a wild goose-chase we'll both be in trouble. I don't suppose you want to tell me what we would be looking for in Ritchie's office?"

"I don't see why not, Agent Gonzalez. I expect to find jewelry-making tools and probably some diamonds too," said Molly in a studiously modest voice.

"And if we find that, the case is solved?"

"If we find that, the case is solved. But we have to discuss how we go about confronting Mr. Ritchie. May I make a suggestion?"

Molly Miller explained, and Agent Gonzalez listened attentively.

Two hours later they were back in Miami. Gonzalez had brought two colleagues along, both younger men and, like himself, not uniformed. His former gloom had been replaced by cautious optimism. Hearing the latest news from Daphne and Molly had alerted all his innate hunting instincts in him. This was just the push he needed to move this case forward. If Mrs. Miller's hunch was correct, and they usually were, this could be the decisive moment. A few phone calls had given him all the information he needed to set the 'Morales campaign' in action and furnish him with the necessary authority.

They knew that Ritchie liked an early lunch and waited outside the Morales Building in their car until they saw him leave. Then they walked in, showed their warrant to the receptionist, and warned her not to alert anyone to their visit. Gonzalez left one of the young officers with her at the entrance. Everybody else passed quickly to Ritchie's office where they locked the door behind them and began a thorough search.

After only a few minutes they found what they were looking for. In one of the desk drawers, under a false bottom which was easily removed, was hidden a small set of tools: a miniature hammer, a prong clip and padded pincers. There was also a small suede purse that contained a dozen polished and cut diamonds in different sizes.

Gonzalez was pleased, but Molly looked positively triumphant. All the time they had moved quietly. Now they unlocked the room and waited, the men standing on each side of the door while Molly occupied the only chair. Gonzalez remained in the back.

Barely an hour after he had left the auction house Edward Ritchie was back. They heard him walk along the corridor and, as he came into the office and saw them, the blood rushed to his face. He seemed stunned for a moment and then, gathering himself, imperious. "What are you doing here? How dare you break into my office? I'll call the police," he shouted.

With faint amusement Gonzalez stepped toward him and replied, "We are the police."

Ritchie rushed forward, angrily, and only then did he notice the tools and the pouch he had so carefully hidden, now laid out on his desk.

"Do you have any right to search my office and go through my things?" he demanded in a shrill and tightening voice.

"We do, Mr. Ritchie. Here is our search warrant." With these words Gonzalez pulled out a paper and held it so Ritchie could read it. He didn't bother apart from a quick look, leaping behind his desk as though to protect his property.

"Why have you got these jeweler's tools?" the agent asked in a calm voice. "And is it normal for an auctioneer to keep loose diamonds in his desk? If they belonged to a customer surely you would leave them in your safe?"

"They are mine and they are not even diamonds. They're just industrial stones that look like diamonds. Practically worthless. I can show you."

"Yes, I know and for the moment I believe you. But how do you explain these tools?"

"That's very simple. Sometimes I have to check the setting of a gem or I even secure a loose stone."

"Really? I would have thought that goes well beyond an auctioneer's duty. And why do you hide this stuff? – Tell me, why do you buy fake diamonds?"

"That's none of your damned business. It's not illegal."

For the first time Molly's voice could be heard. "Mr. Ritchie, are you familiar with the writings of the author Maupassant?"

"What? Never heard the name," Ritchie grunted.

"Well, Yuri was. And just before his death he seems to have been reading a Maupassant story that played on his mind. A story called "The Necklace" that's to do with fake jewelry."

"So? What's that got to do with me?"

"Everything. Because that's the business you are in – faking jewelry – isn't it? You have been defrauding the customers of this auction gallery for some time."

Ritchie gave Molly a sinister look but failed to stop her.

"This is your little scam. Your typical victim is a Latino from out of town who comes to you with something he obviously doesn't know too much about. You examine it and if you see a nice diamond, with a regular cut, normal size, you tell the owner that sadly not all of the stones are of value. However, you continue, some are, and as the workmanship is good, the piece should sell for an acceptable amount. You keep the jewelry to enter it into the next auction. One evening when everybody has gone home, you take out your tools and replace one or two of the real diamonds with matching fakes that you either already own or go out and buy. The real gems you sell. You never exchange all the stones and you don't do it too often. As long as you don't let your greed take over, you have a steady source of extra money. The buyer knows what he is getting but the seller loses."

Ritchie's fury seemed to have dispersed and he sat now in his chair hunched forward. With a voice that held none of his former bravado he spat out, "You can't prove that."

Molly and Gonzalez looked at each other and now Gonzalez spoke up. "Yes we can. We have all the evidence we need. We have witnesses who will swear that they brought you jewelry set with real gems, only to be told by you they were partly fake."

Gonzalez continued: "We also made the acquaintance of your friend Mr. Chen Kwa Dong. He didn't know your real name; but when we showed him a picture of you from one of your own catalogues, he knew the face immediately. In fact he knows you quite well, doesn't he? You're one of his customers. A buyer of fake stones and a seller of real ones."

There was dead silence in the room. At last Agent Gonzalez leaned forward and said to Ritchie, who had buried his head in his hands, "We have the evidence to link you to the murder of Yuri Poliakoff. Edward Ritchie, you are under arrest."

It seemed he was drawing on his last reserves when Ritchie lifted his head and said in something close to a whimper. "I didn't do it. Why should I have killed him?"

Gonzalez spoke in a very clear voice. "Yuri discovered what you were doing. He didn't want to be involved and told you to stop. You argued. He threatened to go to the police. You threatened him with violence, which he took seriously enough to want to store some evidence of what was going on in a safe place. He had planned to leave it with Ewa, his cousin, in Palm Beach. You fathomed that from the telephone message she left at the office, which also gave you the address where she was staying. You then intercepted him in the Caplan garden. There was a fight. You killed him, and you took the evidence."

The agent took a dramatic pause. Then, with impeccable timing, he broke the silence with three short sentences, delivered in a slow voice, deliberately void of emotion.

"Mr. Ritchie, you wasted your time. Because he'd copied it. There was another tape."

The last words had the effect of an exploding bomb.

Ritchie sprang up, his face red and distorted. "What? Another tape?"

"Another tape," confirmed the agent, turning to his colleague. "Read the man his rights!"

****

Three hours later, with Ritchie's confessional statement given and signed, Gonzalez and Molly drove back to Palm Beach. Molly was tired but victorious. Gonzalez looked pleased but thoughtful.

"Well Agent Gonzalez, it was a great pleasure to work with you again. The worst of the two crimes has been solved. I have high hopes that the pictures will be found one day. But there's one thing I don't understand. How did you know it was a tape that Yuri wanted to give Ewa?"

Gonzalez laughed. "I didn't. It was a trap to get the confession. OK, we had the Chinaman's statement but that would only have helped to bring him to justice for the fraud. The murder was a different matter: no witnesses, no evidence. So I had to resort to … let's say a little deception. I admit, it was a long shot but the result was worth the risk. While you were going through all those magazines in Yuri's apartment, I had more than enough time to reflect on what was in the room. Apart from books. And one of the things I saw was an old-fashioned cassette recorder with a microphone attached. It barely registered at the time, but I went back after you left and found he was in the habit of sending taped letters to his relatives in Europe. I just thought, well, this was a man in the habit of recording his thoughts. Maybe he'd have recorded his fears as well.

"So yes, it was a bluff. But a good one. Almost as good as the one about all these people testifying that Ed Ritchie tampered with their jewelry." Gonzalez didn't seem the slightest bit concerned that a fair amount of trickery was needed to pull off victory, i.e. a confession.

"That was indeed an exaggeration. They haven't surfaced yet but I am sure they exist, and once you track some of them down they'll be only too happy to complain," Molly admitted. "Meanwhile, I take it, Ewa is off the hook?" she asked with a smile.

Gonzalez grinned. "Your darling girl is in the clear. What I would like to know is when and why you started suspecting Ritchie. Will you tell me?"

"Why, certainly. Most people, and I guess that applies even to the police and FBI, think in far too complicated ways. You want the correct explanation for a problem? Find whatever satisfies the criteria of possibility most simply. In this case we had decided that Yuri's trouble had to be work-related because there seemed to be no other area of conflict in his life. Therefore, Ritchie, who was in daily contact with him, was the most likely suspect. The magazines confirmed the kind of clients he was addressing, as well as the kind of business he was doing with them. Not to mention his business with the Gemporium. That Yuri – presumably it was him – circled that advertisement was lucky.

"Don't laugh, Mr. Gonzalez, but we women are immediately alerted at the mention of diamonds. Dollar signs flash up in our minds, at least in mine, followed by a notion of danger, even crime. I was intrigued when I saw the copies of Rapaport lying around and began searching them for clues. I admit I was incredibly lucky to hit the right page."

Molly paused. She felt it was time to let Gonzalez in on the action. After all he had contributed his fair share to the successful outcome.

"I must say, you drew your own conclusions pretty quickly the moment we discovered the tools and stones. It was much better that the accusations came from you rather than me. Nobody, at least not a hard-boiled criminal, takes a little old lady seriously. When a man like you speaks up, someone like Ritchie is easily intimidated."

This was as close to flirtation as Molly would ever come in her dealings with Gonzalez. He didn't quite swallow her sudden modesty but felt it best to go along with her apart from a token protest.

"Tell me, was Ritchie your main suspect?" she wanted to know.

"Yes he was, but almost by default. Who else was there? I just wanted to dig deeper before confronting him again. After all, there was little danger that he would disappear. But when you blew the trumpet for attack," Gonzalez allowed himself a little smile at this unlikely metaphor, "I decided to go for it. And luckily it all worked out.

"As for the Gemporium advertisement – well, it was very fortunate that you spotted it, Mrs. Miller. Though I'd rather credit your eagle eye and intuition. On the subject of which, what does your intuition have to say now about the Caplan robbery? Not connected?"

"I don't think so. Again, there is no point in trying to establish convoluted links between the robbery and the murder. Two crimes happened in one night at the same place and we'll have to call it coincidence, fluke. Or synchronicity, to quote Mr. Jung," said Molly.

"Remember, Daphne's neighbor thought she heard three cars that night. This supports my theory: The first to arrive was probably Yuri, let's say at about 10 or a little later. Then Ritchie arrived and confronted him. And unconnected with that, most likely much later, someone else turned up to steal the pictures, with or, less likely, without the help of someone inside the house - although I don't as yet see how a stranger without knowing the alarm combination could manage that."

"Well, it's too bad our art thieves are still at large. But we have our killer – thanks largely to you Mrs. Miller. I'm afraid that, for the time being, the only way I can thank you is to get you over to the police in Palm Beach for some more paperwork. Could you be free tomorrow morning?"

"Paperwork," said Mrs. Miller. "Not the world's greatest reward, but I'll be happy to oblige. What time?"

180

Chapter 18

When she was a child, Molly Miller — who was then Molly Brockmann — hated Sundays because they were boring and overshadowed by the dreaded return to school next day. But Sundays had now become her favorite part of the week. She liked a structure to her life. And while structure had been easy when Jim (who enjoyed organization) was still alive, it was harder now. Except for Sundays, which retained some semblance of an imposed order.

It began with church in the morning: a spiritual as well as social engagement. As a married couple the Millers had supported Bethesda-by-the-Sea, an Episcopal church with a high liturgy whose grandeur was deemed particularly fitting for society weddings of Trump-like excess. But with widowhood, Molly had changed allegiances to the more relaxed Poinciana Chapel: light and cheerful, and blessed with a garden that ran all the way down to Lake Worth.

On Sundays at 10:30 the congregation came together, elegantly attired, ceremoniously ushered in. The Chapel offered a handsome service, not too long and enhanced by excellent music. The proceedings went on with due solemnity until at the very end, when the worshippers roused themselves and burst into a full-strength rendering of *God Bless America* which send many of them out into the world misty-eyed.

Apart from the summer months when major parts of the congregation had left Palm Beach, every service was followed by a meeting in the Fellowship Hall afterwards. Kind lady volunteers served hot and cold drinks, cake, biscuits and savory snacks. Molly's pleasure, however, was marred by just one detail: the coffee was decaffeinated. As a non-smoker who hardly drank, her only vice – if you could call it that – was coffee. But it had to be the real thing: hot, filtered and full of caffeine. "What's the point in drinking coffee if it doesn't give your heart a stir?" she once said to a chapel helper, earning herself a reproachful stare. The average age of the congregation was too high for jests about coronary deficiencies. And as she subsequently learned, the church had just bought a defibrillator.

In the background of the Fellowship Hall a jolly little lady played popular songs on a grand piano, highly conducive to humming and tapping aloud. Air-kissing was abundant. Small groups at round tables drank their emasculated – or as Molly insisted, castrated – coffee and nibbled tidbits. The post-service party was always a great success.

This very agreeable start to the day was usually followed by lunch at the club, always a pleasant affair; and by tea time Molly could congratulate herself on having spent a delightful day. Even if there were no evening engagements, she would return home in a spirit of quiet satisfaction.

Today, though, was a Sunday with the promise of more than usual activity. Molly had been invited with Scott to the opening of a new exhibition at the Norton Gallery in West Palm Beach. It was a social event of some consequence. Everybody who was anybody would be there; and among others, she expected to meet Daphne.

Molly's clothes had been packed ready for the long-delayed departure to Cleveland, and were piled up in the hall ready for collection. Only what fitted into a small suitcase was left hanging in her closet; and from this short supply she now chose a yellow silk suit, one of her favorites. Mr. Miller had always loved her in yellow and the color corresponded with her happy mood today. She had kept this piece back on purpose because she possessed very elegant pumps in the same yellow silk and yes, joy of joys, Mrs. Miller could wear shoes again. The previous day her doctor had taken the bandage off for the last time and declared her healed. He kept her cane and admonished her to walk carefully in future, watching her steps.

Scott was due to leave tomorrow, and however much he had enjoyed spending time with his aunt and taking a rest, he too was now fit and anxious to rejoin the rat race in Manhattan. But until then, nephew and aunt were determined to make the most of their remaining hours together.

When the Norton Museum, one block south of the middle bridge, between South Olive Avenue and South Dixie Highway, opened in the 1940s it had filled a gap in the life of those who yearn for culture in south Florida. Originally consisting of a Chicago steel-magnate's private collection, it had vastly grown and now staged several temporary exhibitions annually that were never too demanding and, moreover, offered an excellent opportunity for social networking. Fundraising committees had to be formed; meetings were necessary to find sponsors and underwriters; cocktail parties had to be arranged to keep them sweet. And the pinnacle of all this feverish activity was the grand opening.

In the season it would probably be a black-tie affair where chairwomen presided, patrons were honored, speeches made, and the inevitable, all-important photos taken.

Today's event, coming after the season and therefore executed at a lower key, marked an exhibition of paintings by a contemporary Mexican artist. They were all oversized representations of fruit: huge apples, bananas, pineapples and mangoes, portrayed with naturalistic precision in earthy colors. The fruit on most canvasses was unblemished, perfect and lifelike, though in certain cases it was halved or quartered, and with pieces bitten out.

At first glance the pictures looked like photographs: not disagreeable, except for the extremely glossy finish on the canvas. Only when you stepped close did you notice that tiny little maggots wormed their way in and out of the fruity flesh. No doubt this unsavory addition was meant to give the paintings deeper meaning. To labor the point they had been given titles like Sic transit Gloria mundi or Memento mori. And taking their cue, the more gullible of the Palm Beach intelligentsia were walking around the room earnestly discussing the artist's insights into the condition of mankind.

A fair crowd had already assembled by the time Molly and Scott arrived. Molly's buttercup-yellow ensemble attracted many admiring glances and several of her friends came over to congratulate her on her recent recovery. It wasn't long before she spotted Daphne who had, as so often these days, her 'girls' with her. Lucinda's chosen T-shirt, half hidden under a pink blazer, admonished the reader Don't copy me! An apt warning in an art gallery, thought Molly.

While Lucinda remained true to her own style, Ewa continued to show encouraging little signs of improvement in her appearance. Gone for good, it seemed, were the plaits, and her old overall had once again been traded for more flattering garments: a blue skirt with a matching top. It wasn't the height of elegance and she had still some weight to loose, but she seemed to be on the right track. Molly looked at Daphne with a nod to Ewa; and Daphne gave her in response a proud and happy smile.

Before she could comment, the imposing figure of Stephen van Dreesen approached, bearing four glasses of champagne. He

184

handed three of them to Daphne and the girls and with a flourish presented the last one, which had presumably been meant for himself, to Molly. "Delighted to see you again, dearest Molly. I do hope you will allow me to call you Molly. An enchanting name, it has always been one of my favorites."

After such attentiveness she could hardly refuse the proffered drink. Scott immediately volunteered to fetch another two glasses, while Stephen took up what was clearly meant to become a permanent position, close to Daphne. Molly noticed that he wore another of his elegant linen suits that never seemed to crumple. This one had a pale olive tinge and was teamed with a matching shirt, olive and white stripes, and a rather daring tie resplendent with green, blue and pink swirls.

They walked around and scrutinized the pictures, struggling to turn out well-informed, intelligent remarks. Van Dreesen was in his element as he seized the chance to impress four ladies. In a booming basso profundo he led his little group of disciples around the rooms expounding on the powerful influence of tribal art in what they saw.

"These still-lifes — as such they are, for want of a better description- bear the crystalline structure and accents of subdued color that mark the transition from analytic to synthetic realism", he revealed, adding that "through the delicately balanced coordination of eye, mind, hand and heart" they "reached into the darkest recess of the soul."

Molly noticed Ewa's exchange of rolling eyes with Lucinda, who also did something unappreciative with her tongue. If van Dreesen's lecture was meant to display his scholarship and erudition he had failed: conspicuously with the youngsters, quietly with Molly too.

Daphne alone listened with encouraging raptness; but then she always had a weakness for van Dreesen's bluster, which she apparently read as charisma. Molly took a few tentative steps aside in an endeavor to make her own way around the room. This was successful since the two girls and Scott moved along together, and Daphne was in thrall to the lecture.

But as she stood in front of one of the paintings, contemplating the compositional importance of a giant apple, she began to feel uncomfortable – and for reasons that had little to with tribal cultures or the recesses of souls. She had been over-ambitious to wear high heels for the first time in weeks and leave her cane behind. Molly limped aside and leant for a moment's respite against a conveniently positioned column, when she heard a voice.

"Do you like it?" asked a woman close by, who had evidently been watching her.

"I am not sure," answered Molly honestly, "I certainly don't dislike it; but if you mean: would I hang it in my room... the answer would be no."

The woman smiled. "What do you hang in your room, if you don't mind my asking?"

"I don't mind. I don't have sophisticated tastes but, as they say, I know what I like. I inherited some English and French 19th century watercolors that I enjoy. I have some family portraits, oil paintings, charming but of no great value. And my husband and I bought some Mexican and Balinese art during our traveling days."

"Hmm, an eclectic mixture. Excuse me, but I noticed that you looked troubled a moment ago. Can I help? Would you like to sit down?"

Molly blushed, explaining about her foot and that this was her first trip out in normal shoes. She ended by introducing herself.

"I am very pleased to meet you, Mrs. Miller," answered the woman. "My name is Marian Bevan and I work here at the museum as a curator — though I didn't put this exhibition together, so today I am here almost as a visiting guest. Now, would you like to come with me and sit down for a while? My office is not far from here."

Molly sighed with relief. "That is wonderfully kind of you, Mrs. Bevan. I'll gladly take up your kind offer."

She followed her new friend into a light and airy room, a floor above, and was about to sink into one of the inviting arm-chairs there when Mrs. Bevan bent down and with a quick "Excuse me" retrieved something from the seat.

The woman, who now sat opposite her, was probably in her forties, her long dark hair tied together with a red scarf that matched her short red skirt. She was pretty, well-dressed and spoke with the kind of strong southern accent that Molly always loved. She noticed that the woman still held what looked like a torch-light in her hand, and commented on it.

"Oh that," said Marian Bevan with a laugh, "That's my blue light. Everybody who works in the art world, I mean with paintings, has one. It's a useful gadget. You pass it over a can-vas and it shows where the picture has been restored or over-painted: a little like an x-ray machine in miniature. Before I came downstairs I was checking out some new things we just got in."

"How fascinating," exclaimed Molly. "So you can see whether the artist has added later to an existing picture or made changes?"

"Absolutely. And where another painter may have come along and made the changes. It happens."

"Why would they do that?" asked Molly. "Sounds like cultural skullduggery."

"Not necessarily," said Mrs. Bevan. "Painters may end up rich but they often start out poor. And materials are expensive.

So it's not uncommon for them to re-use canvasses, painting over what's already there. Or on the back of what's already there. This little light reveals all."

Molly remained silent for a moment. Then she said with genuine gratitude "I cannot thank you enough – both for your concern and for your information. Your little light is fascinating, but I think I'd better get back to my friends. I hope we'll meet again."

"I hope so too," replied the curator pleasantly. "Ask for me any time you are here."

Molly found her group without problems. Having had their fill of art, they had moved out into the courtyard to be closer to the bar. There was another couple with them now, both with dark hair, dressed in black, which was all Molly could see because they stood with their back to her. When she drew closer the man turned around and she recognized Emilio Gonzalez.

"Heavens to Betsy," she exclaimed, "Agent Gonzalez! What a surprise and how delightful to see you here!"

He smiled at her a little self-consciously and replied: "The pleasure is mine, Mrs. Miller. May I introduce to you my wife? This is Teresa. Teresa, this is Mrs. Miller, the lady you've heard so much about."

Teresa Gonzalez was a perfect match, physically, for her husband. Tall and a little heavy, she had ultra-black, short hair with dark eyes under bushy eyebrows that almost met in the middle. To an art-conscious observer she might have resembled Frieda Kahlo. And in the present company there was doubtless someone, somewhere making the comparison.

Molly couldn't resist asking the agent: "Do you come here often? I didn't know you were an art lover."

He shook his head. "Not really. But let's say I've become intrigued as a result of our latest case, Mrs. Miller. In the course of duty I started doing some research in Miami and found an unexpected interest. So I persuaded Teresa to come over and see what was happening here."

"Well, Ms. Gonzalez, you must be very proud of your husband," interjected van Dreesen, assertively gracious as ever. "I'm sure you have heard all about this murder case that he solved so brilliantly. With a little help from our friend here," he added with a wink at Molly.

Instead of Teresa, the agent himself answered. "Yes, thank God we seem to have sorted that one out. And I'm only sorry, Miss Ewa", he said, turning to the girl, "that these last weeks have been so unpleasant for you. Not only have you lost your new-found cousin, and in such a cruel way, but for a time you were suspected of involvement in that loss. I just hope you will overcome these dark days with the resilience of youth."

That was quite a little speech, thought Molly: well put, almost poetic. Who would have thought an FBI agent had such language.

Ewa, who had been cheerful until now, was visibly shaken by the reference to Yuri's death. Daphne saw tears welling in her eyes and took the initiative.

"Ewa, I know you like modern architecture. This museum is one of the most attractive exhibition spaces I know. Why don't you walk around and see the garden at the same time? Scott, this might interest you too, maybe you'd like to accompany her?"

The young man willingly took Ewa's arm and off they went. A little heavy-handed, that, thought Molly; but it served the purpose. Ewa could recover her composure and enjoy Scott's company at the same time. He was a dear boy and could only be delightful company for a young woman, of that the proud aunt was sure.

Daphne turned with a smile to Gonzalez and said: "It's easier to talk about the murder without Ewa. There was one thing I don't understand and maybe you can tell me. Why didn't Yuri, when he discovered Ritchie's fraud, go straight to the police?"

"That's just what I wanted to know myself", Gonzalez said. "According to Ritchie — and I tend to believe him — it all started with an accident. They had a precious ring in custody at the auction house, and the day before the sale they noticed that somehow one of the stones had fallen out and gone missing. The two men, Yuri and his boss, were worried; and to avoid embarrassment they decided to replace the lost gem with a man-made stone. The deception worked, the ring sold, and the problem passed.

"But it excited Ritchie to see how easily this sort of fraud could be carried out and he continued cheating in the same way. When Yuri got wise to the fact that this was becoming regular practice, he tried to intervene. But Ritchie was by now earning too much out of the deception to stop. Yuri didn't want to go to the police because he was implicated in that first fraud, but he did try one more time – unsuccessfully — to make Ritchie come to his senses. Then Yuri told him that he had taped their conversation, together with a full statement, and he threatened to take it to the police if the scam didn't end. In the meantime he would keep the tape in a safe place."

"Poor, silly boy," said Molly. "And for that he died. I guess he didn't think his boss would hold out, or resort to such desperate measures. But there it is: one case solved, although the file on the robbery is still open and we can only wait and see. Ms. Gonzalez, you must be glad this homicide investigation is all over. I guess you haven't seen much of your husband lately."

"Yes, it's good to have him more at home, until the next case comes along," Teresa replied. And from the way she then took her husband's hand tenderly in her own, it appeared that the marital problems to which Gonzalez had once, very cautiously, made passing reference had been dealt with it. Whatever was happening between them a few weeks ago, they now looked, Molly thought, like newlyweds on honeymoon.

Curious as always, she hoped that Gonzalez might take the opportunity to say something about this in private. And the chance came soon enough, as once again she moved away from the group. Gonzalez followed her.

"I'm thrilled to meet your wife, Mr. Gonzalez," Molly sparkled. "She's delightful. You're a lucky man."

A smile of utter happiness transformed Emilio's usually doleful face. As if he had been waiting for his cue he said: "I know that. She is a wonderful person and we are very happy. In fact I have some news for you, very confidential for the moment."

He looked around as if afraid to be overheard by enemy forces. Then Gonzalez bent close to Molly and whispered: "My wife is four months pregnant. By Christmas we'll have a baby."

"Goodness gracious me, Agent Gonzalez, that's the best news I've heard in a very long time!" exclaimed Molly. "You must be ecstatic. If I recall, you've been married for some time and never had any children."

"Yes, when we married we expected them, but then nothing happened. We weren't particularly disappointed because we both have busy lives: my wife's accountancy practice is growing fast, and me – well, you know how my life is. But I'd become concerned about our relationship. Teresa, as I think you know, became withdrawn and showed no interest when I wanted to talk to her, wanted to involve her. I was getting desperate. And then suddenly, last week, she told me the news. She'd been quite apprehensive about it, thinking she was too old for a baby. But that's nonsense. She'll be an excellent mother."

"And you'll be a great dad, Mr. Gonzalez," echoed Molly. "I couldn't be happier for you both. Please convey my heartfelt congratulations to Ms. Gonzalez. And I hope that when the time comes I'll be allowed to see the baby."

"You definitely will. I'll be in touch with you at Christmas."

An hour later Scott was ready to drive his aunt home, returning from the architectural excursion which both he and Ewa evidently found diverting. As usual, he dropped Molly off at the entrance to 325 South Ocean Boulevard while he carried on to the garage.

Felicitously, Robert was on duty and Molly remembered to ask him about her ailing neighbor, Lillian Sorenson, as she still thought of her. The moment he heard the name his face tensed "Oh, you don't know?" he asked. "Well, Ms. Markham has been moved into the nursing home. Mr. Markham tells everybody that he will miss his wife desperately but that the move is for her own good. Of course, he is very lonely in that big apartment all by himself. I suppose that's why a young lady friend has moved in, to keep him company. And now he has started redecorating, in a big way … ripping the kitchen and bathrooms out and replacing them with high-tech appliances, all marble and power jets."

"What, already?" asked Molly horrified. "But his wife has only just gone and she might come back."

"I don't think Mr. Markham is expecting her back. He lives here as if his wife had never existed. In a few weeks time he'll have eradicated all traces of her. You know how in the Soviet Union they eliminated people from photographs who had politically fallen in disgrace? They were simply erased from the picture, or painted over, so you didn't know they'd ever been there."

"Painted over?" Molly seemed distracted for a moment. "I've just been talking about that very subject to a curator at the museum. I can see it's something I shall have to think about a little more."

CHAPTER 19

You could hardly choose a better place or time to launch a project than New York in the week before Christmas – a time when shops are overrun with customers, restaurants with diners and performances with patrons. At no other point in the year do New Yorkers work or play quite so hard. And at no other point are they so robustly on the look-out for new ways to do it.

This was the time, Stephen van Dreesen had decided, to launch his great project – the realization of a long-cherished dream – and stun the international art market into mute submission. Two months earlier, after decades of fringe dealings in cities respectable and rich enough but not exactly the center of the world, he had opened his Manhattan gallery, initially with modest fanfare but now, as planned, with the biggest noise he could muster: the unveiling of a totally unknown Picasso, found and rescued from obscurity by Stephen van Dreesen himself.

The invitations — handsome, heavy cards embossed in gold and black — had gone out, informing the fortunate recipients that on the 19th December, between six and eight pm, the new Picasso would be on public display for the first time. And van Dreesen was more than gratified by the buzz this information had created. Since the first article had appeared in Art World Today by the respected art historian and Picasso scholar

Francis Ogilvy Thorpe, the telephone had hardly stopped ringing. Newspapers, collectors, academics... everybody wanted a share in this particular action. And that the painting had been identified as a 'superlative' example of the artist's youthful work – unequivocally signed and dated in the right-hand bottom corner: Picasso 1905 – intensified the excitement into frenzy.

Van Dreesen had taken the trouble to insert extracts from the Ogilvy Thorpe appreciation along with the invitations. So his guests had been reminded that 'the early works in the long life of this most versatile of visual artists are often considered, by the general public but also many connoisseurs, to be among the artist's most glorious achievements.' This was, as Thorpe continued, 'the period when the young Spaniard's palette shifted in predominance from blue to rose, before his move into what we now call Cubism: a development that reflects the changes taking place in Picasso's life. In 1905 he was introduced to Gertrude Stein and in her circle he began to meet people of influence, to win recognition, and to sell his work. The year before he had met Fernande, the first woman with whom he would share his life, his lover and muse for years to come.'

The painting that evoked such universal curiosity showed a naked woman leaning against a curtain beside an open terrace door. She wore nothing but a pair of red boots and had a white shawl hanging casually from one shoulder. Her dark hair was piled up on her head, her face painted — dark eyes, red lips — and she looked straight at the viewer without a hint of shyness. She didn't quite have the chalky white, elongated body of so many of Picasso's early nudes but was still pale: a beautiful, seductive dark-haired beauty, who proudly showed off her well-proportioned, sensuous body. It was a tall painting, portrait size, 40 x 50 inches.

The provenance of this masterpiece was, by all accounts, a mystery. It had never been seen before but was authenticated beyond doubt. The leading Picasso authorities in London and New York had examined it, as had the directors of the Picasso Museums in Paris and Barcelona, and they had unanimously declared it genuine. Everyone agreed that the painting was a portrait of Fernande, whom the young Picasso had met at the Bateau Lavoir, the ramshackle boarding house in Montparnasse shared by the artist with a number of his fellow-painters.

Experts and critics who had so far seen the picture had been lavish in their praise: sensational discovery, outstanding work of the century, most beautiful early Picasso, masterpiece sans pareil ... and the discovery had made headlines.

Next to photographs of the painting, a beaming van Dreesen had been depicted on the pages of magazines and newspapers throughout the world – alongside estimates of the picture's value, which reached as high as fifty million dollars. The art market was booming and expectations for this new painting were high.

Needless to say, no one had declined van Dreesen's invitation to the viewing. Clients, art lovers, collectors and socialites were forming orderly queues. Van Dreesen was jubilant. Tonight at last, he and his gallery were the talk of the town. From now on his name would be mentioned together with that of Bill Aquavella and the Wildenstein brothers in the big league of dealers. Auction houses would court him, collectors would turn to him. Bigger premises might be necessary. But that was in the future.

Tonight was the time to enjoy his triumph to the full. After thirty-two years in the business, he had hit the jackpot. And as for the demands to know where he had found this picture – let them wonder, let them wait. It was rumored that he had discovered it in an attic in New York, at a Parisian flea market, encrusted in dirt at a provincial Irish auction, in a private house in Peru. Wild conjectures were grist to the gossip mills. So much the better.

A steady flow of limousines deposited his guests at the brightly lit entrance to the gallery. TV crews pressed against uniformed guards on the red carpet. By 6:30 the rooms were almost full. Gus Reuben, who had been entrusted with the display, had done them proud. For this occasion all the walls had been painted black and the only decorations were huge bunches of white lilies in oversized glass vases. The lighting was subdued, with small spotlights illuminating various other pictures – which tonight might as well have been wallpaper in frames for all the attention they drew. The only thing people had come to see was the Picasso which had been enthroned – the only word for it – on a spotlit dais. Presiding magisterially over the room.

The gallery staff tried to keep the visitors moving to allow everyone close access to the picture, at least for a short while. But it was a hard task. Even those with no particular interest in the visual arts seemed captivated – either by the picture or the hype. And as they stood and stared, bus boys in tight black T-shirts with the words van Dreesen gallery emblazoned on the back served white lady cocktails in frosted glasses with a sugar rim – in celebration of the lady on the canvas. The finger-food was Oriental, unidentifiable bits on bamboo trays decorated with orchids.

Having spent the first twenty minutes near the entrance to greet his guests, van Dreesen had now taken up a permanent position close to the painting. With a happy smile he acknowledged the proffered worlds of congratulation, admiration and praise.

Dr. Reuben and some young helpers remained near the door, receiving newcomers and bidding farewell to those who left.

By eight o'clock the waiters had stopped serving and the guards were politely encouraging people off the premises. Van Dreesen was exhausted but overjoyed. The evening had been everything he had hoped for. A small group of friends had gathered in a corner where black leather chairs offered relief to weary feet. Daphne, generous as ever, had invited her friends to a celebratory dinner following the viewing and had urged Stephen and Gus to accompany them to the 21 Club.

Van Dreesen sank into an empty chair and looked around. Now that the tension of the last few hours had subsided, he was happy to see familiar faces and noticed — somewhat belatedly — how elegantly dressed his friends were. Daphne, in a well-cut black suit, congratulated him yet again on the success of the evening. She was accompanied by her stepson Paul and his wife Sarah, who seemed the worse for wear, judging by the glassy look she cast across the room and a faintly bored 'Oh well, so what' expression that betrayed an evening focused on the drinks tray. Meanwhile her husband, habitually eager to please and with an empty, frozen smile on his face, had taken it on himself to make sure that everybody was amply supplied with alcohol and canapés.

On Daphne's other side van Dreesen recognized her charming friend Molly Miller.

Molly, a picture of soignée elegance, had chosen a two piece outfit in reddish-brown silk which suited her brown hair and eyes particularly well. She appeared excited and in high spirits. "Mr. van Dreesen, what a wonderful evening that was! You must be pleased!"

Daphne raised a white lady in salute: "Stephen, my dear, this is to you! I'm only glad to have known you before you became the über-dealer you are now. I guess from here on I won't be able to afford you any more." The company laughed at this small joke, knowing that even the most extravagant Picasso would not be beyond reach of Daphne Caplan's ample trust funds.

"Deborah! I was looking for you," Daphne called across to Deborah Ferolito. "Come and join us. Stephen, you'll remember Deborah, Sol's former secretary? I brought her along to see your treasure."

"I'm so glad you could come," replied van Dreesen who had risen to give a formal bow in her direction. "I hope you were not disappointed."

Deborah Ferolito shook her head, stepping aside to let an attractive young couple enter the circle.

"May I introduce my friends Marylou Baker and Sam Robertson," said Molly. "They have a gallery in Palm Beach and were longing to see the picture, so I asked them as my guests" – adding quickly "of course I telephoned the gallery first and asked permission. And I hope I am not giving a secret away when I tell you that Sam and Marylou are also looking for a place in New York, or possibly Long Island, to open a second gallery."

"No secrets at all," said Marylou. "You set high standards, Mr. van Dreesen, but we think a gallery in Long Island for the summer months when Florida is so quiet makes economic sense. And we're thrilled about the Picasso: it's good for the market, good for us all. How did you find it, dare I ask the question on every lip?"

"Ah... I'm not ready to say yet. But please let me know if I can help in any way when you're setting up here," answered van Dreesen with his usual bonhomie. "I'm all for healthy competition."

"Thank you for allowing us to see your wonderful picture," said Sam. "From now on we will leave no stone unturned until we find our own Picasso. Or at least a new Rembrandt.

200

After six years of running our gallery, Marylou, it's about time you turned up a forgotten masterpiece."

"Well there are problems", she replied to Sam's good-natured reproach. "Starting with the fact that there are no basements and very few attics in Palm Beach as a deposit for undiscovered artwork. Give me an attic, I'll find you a Rembrandt."

Next to her, van Dreesen saw a young girl who seemed vaguely familiar. She had thick, long brown hair and under her blazer he could just read the message on a T-shirt reading: Go with the flow. It rang bells. Had she been around in Palm Beach earlier this year?

This was immediately confirmed by Daphne. "Stephen, I brought along my goddaughter, Lucinda. You may remember that she was my house-guest last summer. Lucinda is a student at Parsons School of Design and obviously she is very interested in modern art."

"Well, young lady," responded Stephen with a smile. "What do you think about the picture?"

Lucinda looked uncertain but rose to the occasion. "Well, this seems to be a very fine example of the early Picasso style. Although I personally prefer his abstract work."

Good humoredly van Dreesen answered. "Well, I am sorry I have nothing of that to show you, but if something turns up in the future I'll let you know."

Daphne thought everybody was ready to go. "What do you think? Are we done? Shall we go? I must say I am rather hungry."

Molly looked nervously at her watch. "I am so sorry, my nephew was supposed to join us. But as he's not here yet, perhaps …"

Her words were interrupted by a loud hammering on the entrance door which had been locked. Everybody turned around and saw through the glass a young man in evening clothes, waving his arms and clearly asking for admittance.

"There he is," said Molly. "That's Scott, my nephew. Can we let him in?"

Gus Reuben had already got up to unlock the door. In bounded Scott, followed slowly by a slender, blond, young beauty. Without waiting for his companion Scott came over to Molly and clasped her in a bear hug. He apologized for being late and continued greeting everybody until he finally turned around and waved forward his friend who had shyly stayed behind.

"Come, come!" He took her hand eagerly. "Nobody's going to bite you. You know almost everybody here anyway, Ewa."

At the mention of her name, all eyes turned to the young woman. Daphne rose and hugged her. The others simply stared. It clearly was Ewa, the same flaxen hair, the blue eyes, but what a transformation had taken place! She must have lost at least twenty pounds, her hair was cut in a becoming bob; she was skillfully made up, and her now lovely figure showed to good advantage in a short frilly dress and fashionably high-heeled shoes. Lucinda followed Daphne's example and gave Ewa a welcoming kiss.

At Scott's insistence Ewa gave a smart twirl, showing off her short, flirty skirt and her perfect figure at the same time. Flushed, embarrassed but also pleased with her success, Ewa said hello to everyone and laughed when they all asked the same thing: "What happened?"

"Well, I came to Manhattan and worked very hard. I shared apartment with some young American girls from my institute. They were nice, we got on so well but then, how shall I say, they attacked me."

"What do you mean?" Daphne sounded anxious. "What did they do?"

"No, no." Ewa laughed. "They wanted to help me. They put me on diet; they took me to hairdresser and made me buy make up. Then they took my old things away, dresses and over-alls. But by then I had lost so much weight that I had to buy new clothes anyway. Well, and then Scott came to take me to Frick Museum. When we met in Florida he had suggested to show me because his office is so close. I really had forgotten."

"How could you, Ewa?" interrupted Scott, trying to look disappointed and reproachful. "I certainly had not forgotten my promise. Only when I came to collect her, I didn't recognize her. Wow, I thought, she is not only clever but beautiful too. Anyway, we went to the Frick Collection, and then the Guggenheim, and then the Met...Well, luckily there are enough museums in New York to keep us going for a while."

With a proprietary gesture the young man put his arm around Ewa's shoulder. "When my aunt told me about tonight, I thought it would be fun to bring her along." He was clearly proud of his friend and enjoyed showing her off.

"Well done Scott," said Daphne, "that was a good idea. I must say, this is like being back in Palm Beach. I hope you will all return next year. Do come and stay with me! I had such a good time with you all – it almost made those terrible events worth dealing with. I just hope we'll never see anything like that again. I still haven't replaced the Friesz over the mantelpiece."

"I heard that the other painting, the Blanche Camus has been found. Is that right?" Marylou wanted to know.

"Yes," confirmed Daphne. "It was really strange – almost as though the thieves were giving it back to me. It turned up at the staff entrance of the Metropolitan Museum here in New York, left in some corridor but securely wrapped and with my name attached to it. No one claimed to have seen who left it. The police was called in but, needless to say, got nowhere with their inquiries. As yet, I should say. Apparently Special Agent Gonzalez is still working on the case. He certainly is a tenacious man. Since the insurance company had already paid up for both the stolen paintings, I returned to them the relevant portion of their money and now I have the Blanche Camus landscape back. It's hanging in its former place. I guess after all these months I'll have to learn to live without the other one."

"I am not so sure." These five little words, spoken with noticeable severity by Molly Miller, made everyone look up.

"I don't think your picture has disappeared forever, Daphne. Perhaps it is just hidden."

To everyone's surprise Molly now climbed up on the dais. Van Dreesen stared at her, mesmerized, apparently unable to move. Before anyone could stop her, Molly had pushed the painting slightly forward on its easel and, with the other hand, begun to peel the backing off. Under brown paper was a piece of rough burlap covering the back of the canvas. At this moment van Dreesen roused himself to action. He got up and stepped forward. But some mysterious authority emanating from the short woman above him kept him at a distance. With a half-strangled voice he shouted "No, no!" and stretched out his arms in an imploring gesture. "Stop!"

Marylou and Sam had moved to either side of van Dreesen as if to protect Molly, who showed little emotion, certainly no fear.

"Until this moment I was not certain but now I know." Molly spoke with a clear, soft voice which only underlined the drama of the unfolding events. "What we see here isn't just Portrait of Fernande by Picasso but Reclining Nude by Othon Friesz as well. Isn't that right, Mr. van Dreesen? They have been painted back to back on the same canvas."

The dealer looked aghast. Like a balloon struck by a pin his body collapsed in on itself, he shrunk down into a chair where he buried his head in his hands.

None of the company spoke: they were too stunned for words. Dr. Reuben looked thunder-struck. Even Sarah seemed to have sensed that a bomb had just exploded, although she wasn't sober enough to work out what was happening.

Sam and Marylou swiftly stepped up to the dais and helped Molly remove the paper from the back of the picture. They carefully laid the picture on the floor, face down, and with a big pair or scissors that Gus found them, they cut the burlap off. Rather than the off-white, empty space that should have been revealed, there was another painting. The stolen Friesz.

Daphne leapt to her feet and hugged Molly. She was finding it difficult to speak. Too many thoughts were racing through her head.

"Wow, that's so awesome!" exclaimed Lucinda, who was the first to find words. "It's just like James Patterson's Lifeguard ... Well, not quite." She looked around but nobody responded.

Scott, used to making decisions under pressure, finally took the initiative. "Shouldn't we call the police? It looks like there's a crime to report here."

"Wait a minute, Scott!" Daphne interrupted him calmly, aware now of the pivotal role this new development had given here. "Let Molly explain before we take any further action."

With general agreement, they all sat down again. Molly stepped off the dais with Sam and Marylou, and began.

"I have really been puzzled by the theft of the two paintings from Daphne's house last May. So many people had the opportunity to take the pictures and some certainly had a motive. The thief, or thieves, probably came through the front door. They either had a key or were let in. And either they knew how to turn the alarm on and off or someone did it for them. This is why I, like the police, suspected just about everybody who stayed that night in the house. We heard that Paul and Deborah both sneaked into the study, but not to steal the paintings. Betty the housekeeper came under suspicion and even Ewa through her connection with her poor cousin Yuri. But nothing could be proven and, most importantly, the pictures were not found.

"There were other mysterious circumstances. The thief or thieves must have had inside knowledge. Rather than go for the celebrated Impressionist paintings which would have been almost impossible to sell anyway, he, she or they settled for two pictures of relatively modest value which were not individually alarmed and therefore easier to steal.

"We know that Sol was particularly attached to the Friesz painting. In fact he had stipulated in his will that this picture, and this picture alone, was not to be sold by his heirs. I could not get this piece of information out of my mind. What made this Reclining Nude so special? I didn't understand why Sol with his exquisite taste and – excuse me, Daphne – his propensity for showmanship, had such a relatively minor painting in such a very important place, over the mantel. Something was not quite right there.

"When I read the details that came with my invitation for tonight I noticed that the Picasso had exactly the same dimensions as the Friesz: 40x 50 inches. The only difference was that the Picasso was in portrait format while the Friesz was landscape. Something clicked and I reminded myself of what Sam and Marylou had told me about the painter Othon Friesz when I consulted them after the theft. Do you remember how you mentioned that he had a studio in the same building as Pablo

Picasso, and how poor they were in these days? If you don't mind, please tell us a little more about that."

Without hesitation Marylou took up the thread: "In 1905, when Friesz painted the Reclining Nude he lived in the famous Bateau Lavoir, a big house at Montparnasse that apparently resembled the barges used by washerwomen on the Seine. Other painters had their studios there and one of them was Picasso. Yes, they all were desperately poor in their early days — Picasso once sold ten drawings for 20 francs – and material was relatively expensive and therefore often in short supply. Once, Picasso was obliged to produce a flower-piece without the use of white, that fundamental pigment, because he couldn't afford it. And he would paint one picture over another and then re-stretch the canvas and work on the back. The lovely Fillette a la corbeille fleurie has no less than three superimposed pictures behind: a portrait of a woman, two men in top-hats and a composition of three figures. Is that what you wanted to know, Molly?"

"It is indeed. But there is something else that needs explaining. As I've discovered from doing some background reading, the two men, Picasso and Friesz, were more than colleagues. They shared their meals, their drinks, and their painting material and apart from that their mistresses were sisters. Fernande had moved in with Picasso the year before, and her sister, some say she was an adoptive sister, Antoinette, lived with Othon Friesz.

"Maybe I am a romantic but I visualize a scene when the two couples sit together after dinner, laughing, drinking, talking and Friesz shows the others the latest portrait he just painted of Antoinette. Picasso, ever the showman, inspired by love and perhaps too much wine, wanted to prove that he can do better. He turned the canvas around, re-stretched it and within a short time completed another picture, another nude, this time Fernande.

"We don't know and probably never will, what happened to the double picture and why one side was covered up. Don't forget, a Friesz or even a Picasso in these days was sometimes given away as payment for a good meal.

"Now I fast forward fifty or sixty years. Mr. van Dreesen, forever browsing through auctions, galleries and markets, finds the Reclining Nude. He likes the painting, it is cheap and he tells his new client, Sol Caplan, about it. Rather than wait and let Mr. van Dreesen deal with the purchase, Sol goes and buys it, for very little money, I guess. When he comes home he examines the picture and finds another one on the back of the canvas. He cleans it and discovers Picasso's Fernande. Given a little more time, no doubt Mr. van Dreesen would have done the same but he never had the opportunity. So, in a way he was twice cut out of the deal.

"Most people would have told the world about this amazing double painting. But Sol was different, as you, Daphne, know best of all. He could be secretive. He hated the thought of all the hullabaloo this discovery would have caused. He might well have felt morally obliged to pay something to Mr. van Dreesen who had after all found the painting, if it had become known that there was a second, even more valuable painting, on the other side of the canvas. So, suddenly Sol owned a genuine Picasso but did not need to insure and protect it or share it with the world. For him it was enough, occasionally to take the backing off and enjoy the treasure he owned – for his eyes only. He knew that one day his secret would be discovered, and he thought it was all a great joke. To make sure that the Picasso stayed in the family, he stipulated in his will, that his heir, Daphne, was not allowed to sell the picture."

Molly paused a moment and looked at Daphne, who seemed strained. With a glance at van Dreesen, she spoke now. "I suppose, Stephen, that you discovered the second painting when you valued and cleaned the pictures after Sol's death."

Van Dreesen nodded and then slowly raised his head. "I just want you to know that Gus had no idea, he was not involved in any of this."

"I was almost sure of that," said Molly. "But to continue with my reconstruction of events: Most of this is pure assumption on my part, though in the light of what we've just discovered it is probably the truth. In order to clean the Friesz painting, Mr. van Dreesen removed the backing and to his utter surprise discovered the hidden Picasso. He was thunder-struck. He didn't tell Daphne. He couldn't stop thinking about it. In the end he decided he had to have it. He had never stolen anything before but he justified himself by saying that he had been treated unfairly by Sol. By rights, some of the picture's value should have come to him. It was irresistible for him to take revenge and profit from his luck or talent. He had always dreamed of a gallery in New York and with a genuine Picasso in his possession this ambition would be within reach. He felt that he was not depriving Daphne of anything she was particularly attached to. She didn't know what she was missing out on and could easily find a replacement for the Friesz painting."

Molly paused and then addressed van Dreesen who remained immobile and speechless in his chair.

"How did you do it? I am almost certain you did not come yourself; you needed someone who could immobilize a burglar alarm because you thought that would be necessary. It probably didn't take you long to find an 'expert' for the task. To make it less obvious, the thief was to take both paintings from the study. Entering the house was easy, as you had made a copy of the front-door key during the days you were busy there. You had also supplied some information on the make and type of alarm in the house that would help to disconnect the system.

"On the night in question the burglar parked his car down the road. Daphne's neighbor thought she had heard three cars drive up that night. One was Yuri, one his murderer, Ritchie, and finally the burglar. He walked on the grass borders, avoiding the gravel, to the front door which he opened without problem. He was ready to cut the alarm wire but to his utter astonishment the alarm was not activated. Someone had conveniently turned it off. He took the pictures, left and locked the house, and the next morning handed over the stolen goods to Stephen for whatever price had been arranged. The Blanche Camus was subsequently returned in a strange, necessarily arms-length fashion. Maybe that was conscience. And we know what happened to the other picture."

Molly, getting tired, asked for a glass of water. She was not allowed to rest for long. Everybody urged her to continue with her story.

"Well, where was I? Yes, the alarm. What had happened? Why was the alarm not switched on? As we know, the next morning, when Betty opened the house, the alarm was set as always. Daphne swears that nobody outside the house knew the combination that turned the alarm on and off. Van Dreesen certainly did not know. It would have been most suspicious if he had tried to find out.

"Only a few days ago I discovered the answer to this puzzle. On a hunch I called the Palm Beach police to ask whether any new information had come to light regarding the burglary. Not really, was the answer — except that a cab driver had come forward who claimed that on the night of the burglary he had picked up someone at the Hudsons' house. That's another neighbor. A young woman had booked a ride to a night club. The cabbie had left Palm Beach the next day for a fishing trip to an isolated cabin without TV and had heard about the crime only much later, after his return.

"Well, the police didn't think this had anything to do with the crime. However, dutifully they got in touch with the Hudsons. They, not surprisingly, could not remember whether anyone had used a taxi that night. They did confirm though, that they had a number of young people staying at their house over the summer, coming and going late in the evenings, and they thought it quite possible that one of their guests had used a cab to join other friends at a night club. The police did not think this was a trail worth following.

"However, when the police told me about this, I was intrigued. Indeed, it cleared up the last uncertainty I had about how the crime was committed."

Molly stopped. She looked over to the sofa where, next to Daphne, Lucinda sat. The young girl's head was flushed and her eyes had filled with tears. With a little quiver in her voice she started speaking, at first so softly that one could hardly hear her, then gaining strength.

"I'm so terribly sorry, Aunt Daphne. I should have told you earlier, but I was so ashamed. I just didn't know what to do. I was really frightened. I thought if my father finds out, I'll have to go back to London and he'll send me to a boring English university. I so wanted to be in New York and I was afraid if I spoke the truth, I'd....I'd be punished."

Daphne had put her arm around the girl and this gentle gesture was too much for her. Lucinda burst into tears and buried her head in her godmother's shoulder. Daphne stroked her hair and, with a smile, turned to Molly. "Do you want to tell us what happened?"

"It seems that young Lucinda, who was used to a lively club scene from London, found Palm Beach rather boring. Somehow she must have heard about a nightclub and she decided to go there secretly, rather than ask for permission. So, our enterprising young lady booked a taxi to collect her late at night. Obviously she didn't want the car to drive up to the house, so she gave the neighbor's address, where there was much coming and going of cars last summer.

"Lucinda waited until everybody was asleep, then she tiptoed downstairs and turned the alarm off. She let herself out through the French doors in the study. She slipped through the hedge into the next door garden and waited in the Hudson's drive for the cab to pick her up. A few hours later she returned. I don't know whether she used a taxi again or perhaps, more likely, someone gave her a lift home. She came back into Daphne's house through the terrace door that she had left open. Naturally she did not turn any light on, so she would not have noticed that the two paintings were missing. She switched the alarm back on and went to bed. It was bad luck that she had chosen for her adventure just the night the house was robbed. The burglar, prepared to immobilize the alarm, must have been overjoyed to find that it was not activated."

Molly stopped and in the ensuing silence only Lucinda's sobs and her occasional use of a handkerchief were audible.

Daphne patted the young girl gently. "Now, now, darling, this is not the end of the world. I cannot pretend that I think it a good idea if a young girl in my care goes secretly to night clubs but worse things happen. Unwittingly you made the job easy for the burglar that night but he would still have stolen the paintings, even with an active alarm. Frankly, I don't think your parents need to know about this little escapade of yours. I guess you have learned your lesson. And when you come back to visit me next summer we have to make different arrangements for your nightly amusement."

The girl let out a huge sigh of relief and squeezed Daphne with all the might of an overjoyed teenager. "Oh thank you, Aunt Daphne. You are so wonderful. I will never forget this. And I will never do anything so stupid again." Under the tears that were still coming, Lucinda managed a little laugh and everybody smiled.

Now Scott, newly energized, jumped up, ready for action.

"Daphne, I don't like doing this, but should we not call the police? Whatever our feelings of friendship may be toward Mr. van Dreesen here, he has committed a crime and we can't just pretend that nothing happened. You decide what to do," he added politely.

Daphne looked over to the art dealer who seemed on the verge of break-down. He was shaking now and his face was deadly white.

"Well..." said Daphne, pausing with momentary indecision. "No, I've decided. I cannot bring myself to hand over Stephen to the police. Sol would not have wanted it. They were such good friends. Under normal circumstances Stephen would never have betrayed me, he was always fair and decent in all business dealings with Sol: more so, it seems, than my dear husband was with him in return. I imagine the discovery of the Picasso totally overwhelmed him and robbed him of his sound judgment. Most people act atypically when under stress.

"Also, I don't feel that Stephen has really deprived me of anything. In fact, without him I might have never known about the Picasso and the world would have never, or at least not for a very long time, seen this beautiful painting. I don't think money came much into it for Stephen. It was partly revenge and partly the glory, the triumph over competitors that tempted him. All heady stuff and hard to resist."

She paused for a moment. "Maybe you, Scott, can help us to work something out, whereby I officially buy the Picasso from Stephen — of course for a sum which has to remain undisclosed. I am sure everybody agrees that the picture, Picasso or Friesz, should rejoin the Sol Caplan collection. You and I, Stephen, will share the financial gain from your discovery, but the kudos will remain yours and help your business. We'll have to put things right with the insurance company but that may not be too big a problem. I can tell them the Friesz has been recovered. You, Stephen, can repay them what they paid me out of your fee for the Picasso. I'm sure you won't object to that. And as for the rest … I think we should all keep quiet about what we heard tonight."

It was an impressive and dignified speech that ended with Daphne casting a pointed glance at Paul and Sarah. "Maybe we can come to a financial arrangement that will safeguard everybody's discretion. Let's talk about this tomorrow. Stephen, I guess you are too upset to go out. Maybe Dr. Reuben will be kind enough to take you home."

The young man, himself clearly shaken, came forward and stepped next to his boss.

Daphne got up and took Molly's hand.

"Dearest Molly, you have done it again. I don't know how you solve these puzzles, but I'm grateful that you do. And thank you for providing me with my very own Picasso. What can I say — it's been quite a night! And I don't know about you, but personally I'm starving. Scott, do you think the 21 Club will still take us so late?"

Scott leapt to attention, dragging Ewa with him. "I should think so. Let's go. Too much drama on an empty stomach isn't good for anyone. Not even you, my dearest super-sleuthing aunt. She's quite a woman isn't she?"

214

"The best," said Ewa, holding out her arm to Molly.

"Oh," said Mrs. Miller, "I just like to see loose ends tied up. It's neater. The one thing that worries me is how I'm going to keep this particular bit of neatness from Agent Gonzalez should our paths ever cross again. But then, I don't suppose they will."

"I wouldn't bet on that," said Scott.

ABOUT THE AUTHOR

Dagmar Lowe lives in Palm Beach and London, where she has been a BBC broadcaster and written for the Evening Standard, Daily Telegraph, and Literary Review. A native of Germany and the mother of four, she studied literature and art history at the University of Zurich. Her Molly Miller series of mysteries was introduced with *A FairWay to Die*, and will be continued by SleuthHound Books in the fall 2007 publishing season or as soon as she wraps up an international sleuthing adventure that reportedly has something to do with a lavish wedding in England.

A FairWay to Die:
It Happened in Palm Beach
by Dagmar Lowe

ISBN: 0893344214 (paperback)
$16.95
ISBN: 0893344222 (hardcover)
$26.95

A brutal murder shatters the peace and quiet of the exclusive Evergreen Golf Club in Palm Beach, Florida. A prominent member is found clubbed to death on the fairway. Suspicion falls on his friends, his family and his neighbors on Golfview Road. FBI Special Agent in Charge, Emilio Gonzalez, who investigates the crime, runs into problems. But help is at hand: in the shape of flirtatious widow Molly Miller, Palm Beach's answer to Miss Marple. She knows the scene, she watches her friends…and solves the case.

"It's about time there was a novel about Palm Beach. It is one of my favorite playgrounds and certainly provides a rich and fertile mine for a writer of glamorous fiction, particularly since I feature in it."
--Julian Fellowes, Academy Award winner (Gosford Park*)and author of* Snobs

"Move over Miss Marple! Here comes Molly Miller, a flirtatious widow and accidental sleuth. An insider's description of the Palm Beach social life. I loved it!"
--Lady Carolyn Townshend
Event Organizer, London and Palm Beach

"A whodunnit in the classic mould, but so much more! An exciting story is told with humor and charm. Palm Beach and the social scene are depcicted accurately, as a 'native' I can vouch for it. Well worth reading!"

--Princess Anne Obolensky

"I was amused and entertained by this clever book. If you like Agatha Christie, you'll love this one."

--Judy Schrafft
Journalist and Writer

ORDER TODAY!

A FairWay to Die: It Happened in Palm Beach

by Dagmar Lowe

QTY	ISBN	TITLE	PRICE	TOTAL
	0893344214	A FairWay to Die (PB)	$16.95	
	0893344222	A FairWay to Die (HC)	$26.95	

S & H	
($6.00 for first book, $2.00 for each additional)	
TOTAL	

NAME: _____

ADDRESS: _____

CITY, STATE, ZIP: _____

TEL: _____

CARD NO: _____ EXP: _____

FAX THIS PAGE TO 1-888-874-8844

or go to

www.sleuthhoundbooks.com

Printed in the United States
72558LV00006B/103-123

9 780893 344252